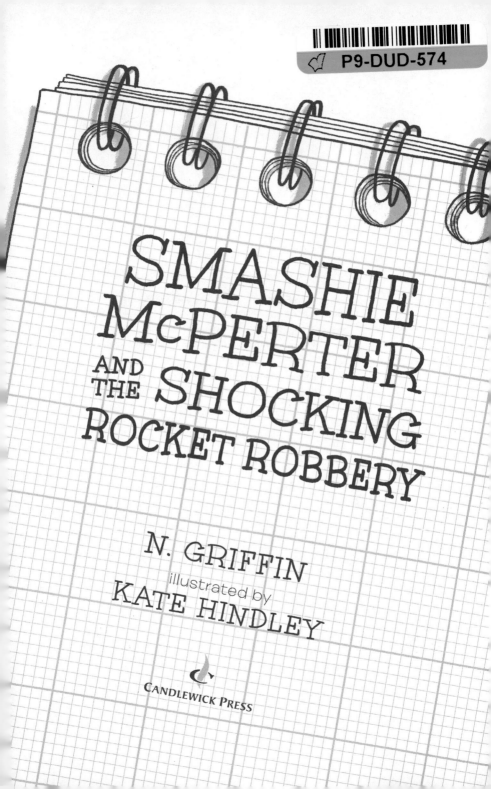

SMASHIE McPERTER
AND THE SHOCKING ROCKET ROBBERY

N. GRIFFIN

illustrated by
KATE HINDLEY

CANDLEWICK PRESS

Text copyright © 2022 by N. Griffin
Illustrations copyright © 2022 by Kate Hindley

First edition 2022

Library of Congress Catalog Card Number 2021935045
ISBN 978-0-7636-9470-8

22 23 24 25 26 27 LBM 10 9 8 7 6 5 4 3 2 1

Printed in Melrose Park, IL, USA

This book was typeset in Dante.

Candlewick Press
99 Dover Street
Somerville, Massachusetts 02144

www.candlewick.com

MIX
Paper | Supporting
responsible forestry
FSC® C103098
FSC
www.fsc.org

SMASHIE McPERTER
AND THE
THE SHOCKING
ROCKET ROBBERY

For Esme and Eamon, of course,
plus T and the gals of BT
NG

For Winnie and Badger
KH

CHAPTER 1
Dangling

It was just before the start of the day at the Rebecca Lee Crumpler Elementary School, and Smashie McPerter was hanging by her knees from the jungle gym on the playground.

"I don't think this is such a good idea," said her best friend, Dontel Marquise.

Smashie and Dontel had so much in common, they were more like cousins than just regular best friends. Both preferred cake to pie and cookies to either. They dipped their french fries in mayonnaise rather than ketchup. And they both loved to think.

Indeed, they had been co-champions of both the lower-school Mathathon and spelling bee last year. This year, in third grade, they had had to think especially hard on two occasions when they were called upon to solve mysteries that had plagued Room 11, their class. In the first, Patches, Room 11's beloved hamster, had gone missing and in the second, a jar of glorious hair goop made by a classmate and her mother had disappeared. Smashie and Dontel had enjoyed being investigators, although the investigations themselves had not always gone smoothly. Still, Smashie's hectic and heartfelt thinking and Dontel's thoughtful and methodical approach complemented each other beautifully, and both cases had been satisfactorily solved.

The two friends also both had grandmothers at home who kept an eye on them after school. This was mostly wonderful, because they loved their grandmothers very much. But it was also hard sometimes, because their grandmothers saw eye to eye on the subject of Smashie and Dontel and were forever squelching ideas that the two children felt were excellent. Like this dangling Smashie was doing right now. She knew instinctively that her grammy would not like her to be dangling from the high bar of the playground jungle gym. Smashie was not at her best with things to do with physical prowess.

Even Dontel was concerned. "You hanging like that, Smashie—I don't know. I don't think you've got the knees for it." He shook his head.

"But I have to," said Smashie, whose knees, in truth, were not feeling so great. "I have to train myself up. If we ever have to be investigators again, we may have to dangle."

"Why would we have to dangle? We never had to dangle when we were investigators before," Dontel pointed out.

It was true. Dangling had been completely unnecessary in either of their previous cases.

But Smashie was firm.

"You never know," she said. "In a lot of the mystery stories I read, the investigators have to dangle to avoid detection. From motion sensors and things."

"First, I think dangling happens mostly with spying, not investigating," Dontel said. "And second, we don't have motion sensors here at the Rebecca

Lee Crumpler Elementary School. Just regular fire alarms and things. If we dangle in front of them, we might set them off by mistake, and I think that would even be illegal."

"I don't mean we should tamper with them!" cried Smashie. "I just mean we have to be ready for anything! And there are spies who are investigators, too, by the way! Spies who also are trying to conquer injustice! Isn't that what we do, when we are investigating? Conquer injustice?"

Dontel extended his arms, clearly readying himself to catch Smashie in case the worst came to pass. "Maybe I could do the dangling for us, if we ever need to dangle," he suggested.

"No," said Smashie firmly. "That wouldn't be fair. I have to do my share." Her upside-down position had made her face very red and her cheeks feel like they were sinking into her eyes. "But I better get down now. The bell for the start of school is going to ring in a few minutes." And she tried to pull herself up to catch hold of the bar with her hands.

There was a lot of grunting.

"I shouldn't grunt so much." Smashie sighed,

her torso and head flopping upside down again. "An investigator can't make that much noise."

"I think you are just excited about investigating and spying for justice because your grammy gave you those hats to play with," said Dontel. "I think you like the idea of using them in a case. I think you want to make an Investigator Suit with them, and that's what all this dangling is all about."

Smashie's face reddened some more. For Dontel was right. Smashie loved making suits. Suits put Smashie in the right frame of mind to solve difficult problems. In the past, she had made a Where Did I Leave My Shoes? Suit and a What Happened to the Fudge I Left Outside to Cool? Suit. In fact, her most successful suits had been the Investigator Suits she had made when she and Dontel had worked to solve those two previous mysteries.

And it was true that Grammy had just given her some very wonderful hats to play with.

"She really meant the hats for both of us to play with," said Smashie. "But you've been so busy this week after school, you haven't even come over!"

It was true. The two friends lived across the street

from each other and played together nearly every day after school. But not this week.

"I can't help it," said Dontel, shifting a bit where he stood. "I've had a lot to do."

"So you say," said Smashie. "But I have to admit, I started playing with the hats without you."

"That's okay," said Dontel. "It's not your fault I couldn't come over."

"Don't forget Grammy gave me a pretend mustache for us to play with as well, Dontel." Smashie's voice wobbled a bit. It was clear her knees were wearing out. "We can use that and the hats to alter our appearances in case we have to spy on suspects and report on their movements without being recognized!"

"Smashie," Dontel said, "everyone would know it was us because of those hats. You shared them during morning meeting yesterday." He shook his head. "I think you ought to be more careful about bringing in stuff from home to share. You never know who's going to do what with it."

"I think you are just nervous because of the things that happened the other week," said Smashie.

The things that had happened the other week were not good, and they were all to do with Brainyon.

Brainyon was Smashie and Dontel's favorite action hero. He was not the kind of superhero who had magic superpowers. Instead, he used the power of his mind to invent things and his own hands to make them. Smashie and Dontel both liked him so much they had black Brainyon backpacks and matching Brainyon T-shirts. And on one fateful day the other week, Dontel had brought in his new Brainyon action figure to share during morning meeting. Billy Kamarski, their classmate and a born prankster, grabbed it right out of Dontel's hand and positioned it on the rug as if it'd been flattened by Billy's own action figure of The Haddock, his favorite supervillain. Billy was not alone in his love for The Haddock. The Haddock was their classmates Joyce Costa and Charlene Stott's favorite action star, too. Unlike Brainyon, The Haddock had fishlike superpowers that he used to triumph over others. He blew dense bubbles with his gills to stupefy those who would stop him, for example, and created water spouts to drag other, good superheroes into the ocean, where he knew his superpowered fish tail would help him outswim them. Billy spent the whole day swiping the Brainyon action figure from Dontel and positioning

it in different poses of defeat under the finny tail of The Haddock.

And then finally, and worst of all, Billy defaced a picture Dontel drew of a space-suited Brainyon that day in art class. Billy scrawled the gill-laden head of The Haddock over the face of Brainyon on the picture. That had done it, both for Smashie and Dontel and for Ms. Early, their teacher. She confiscated Billy's fishy action figure for the rest of the day and forbade Billy from bringing it into Room 11 for two whole weeks.

Even Joyce and Charlene had to admit that it was a fair comeuppance. Still, ever since, Dontel had not drawn a single Brainyon picture and refused to bring in things to share during morning meeting.

But Smashie still loved to share. And just yesterday she had shared the three hats Grammy had given her with the class. One was big, Russian, and furry; one was a homburg with the letters AAM embroidered shakily on one side; and one was scarlet turban made of satin with a pretend jewel positioned in its center front.

"People loved my hats!" Smashie cried now. "My

grammy had them freshened up specially for us to play with! They belonged to her from her theater days!"

"Better that than her go-go dancing days," said Dontel, who did not like to think about those days at all.

There was a terrible thump. Smashie had fallen to the ground at last.

"Ow," she said, and slapped her palms together to get the dirt off them. They stung.

"Maybe you ought to do the dangling next time," she said to Dontel, "and I will pay attention for pointers."

"It's a deal." But who could have known that Smashie would be called upon to test her terrible skills at dangling during the course of this very day? Neither Dontel nor Smashie. But so it was to be.

The yard lady, Miss Martone, blew her whistle just as the bell rang to signal the start of the school day. Dontel and Smashie were glad, because Room 11 was about to embark on an adventure they had been looking forward to for weeks.

CHAPTER 2
Field Trip!

C. DuVASSE BRYSON

"Can you believe we finally get to go to the planetarium today?" Dontel cried as the children put away their belongings.

"No," said Charlene, jigging up and down. "I can hardly wait!"

"Me too," agreed John Singletary. "I love field trips!"

"Gets us out of schoolwork," said Billy Kamarski.

"Circle up, children!" Ms. Early clapped her hands. "Quickly!"

It was unusual for Ms. Early to hurry them along

so firmly. But this was no ordinary day. Room 11 was going to have morning meeting and a brief recess right away, and then, after that, they were leaving for the planetarium! Dontel had been pestering Ms. Early for the class to do a unit on astronomy for weeks now and, at long last, they were starting that unit today, kicking things off with this visit to the planetarium in the city nearby.

Smashie and Dontel were both excited, but Dontel most of all. It was his dream to grow up to be an astrophysicist. His idol was Cornelius duVasse Bryson, noted astrophysicist and head of the Blayden Planetarium, in faraway New York City. Dontel had all of Dr. Bryson's books, and one was even a special autographed copy his grandma had given him for his birthday last year. Dr. Bryson's oeuvre was Dontel's most prized set of possessions.

"As I said yesterday, this will not be like our normal morning meetings," said Ms. Early.

"Darn," said Billy. "I wouldn't mind another look at Smashie's hats. Those were cool. Especially that homburg."

Even though Billy could be something of an unreliable prankster, Smashie beamed.

"Smashie's hats were very interesting," agreed Ms. Early. "But today we need to talk about our field trip. I want you know just what to expect."

"Exhibits!"

"Activities!"

"A space-related snack!"

Ms. Early nodded. "All those things are going to happen," she confirmed.

"I bet you want to go over the rules with us, too, Ms. Early," said Tatiana Navarro, "so we behave the way you expect us to."

"You're right," said Ms. Early. "Let's talk about that together now and make a list of guidelines." She uncapped a marker to write Room 11's suggestions on a piece of chart paper. By the end of the conversation, Room 11 had five rules on their list:

RULES FOR ROOM 11
ON OUR FIELD TRIP:

1. Stay in your seats when the bus is moving.
2. Be respectful to people at the planetarium.
3. No running in the planetarium.
4. Stay with the group.
5. Listen to the chaperones.

Billy Kamarski slumped.

"Can't we have any fun on this trip?" he moaned.

"We will have fun," said Ms. Early firmly. "But we will behave in a way that reflects well on our class and the Rebecca Lee Crumpler Elementary School community." She set down her marker and turned to the class. "Room 11," she said, "do you remember who our chaperones are going to be?"

Dontel and Smashie exchanged pleased smiles.

"Smashie's grammy," said Charlene.

"And Dontel's grandma, too," said Jacinda Morales.

"Exactly!" said Ms. Early. "We are very lucky Mrs. Tango and Mrs. Marquise were available to join us." Mrs. Tango was Smashie's grandmother, and Mrs. Marquise was Dontel's. Both women had been so excited by the idea of a trip to the planetarium that they had volunteered to chaperone. Smashie was sure it had nothing to do with keeping an eye on her and Dontel. Fairly sure, anyway.

As if on cue, a knock came on Room 11's door. Alonso Day opened it, and there stood the two grandmothers, smiling.

"Hello, Room 11!" they cried. Mrs. Marquise carried a large tote bag, and Smashie knew that inside it was a large plastic container holding a special space-related snack for Room 11 to eat on the trip. But the nature of the snack was a surprise for the class. Smashie and Dontel knew what it was because they had helped make it. At first, Smashie hoped she and Dontel and their grandmothers would prepare tubes of astronaut food, but she was glad in the end they had not, since tubed supper sounded like a fairly blucky snack to her, if she was honest. And the treats they *had* made to surprise their class were pretty wonderful.

"Class, say hello to Mrs. Tango and Mrs. Marquise," said Ms. Early. "And thank them for the treats they've brought. We'll stop at a rest stop to eat them on the way to the planetarium."

"Good morning, Mrs. Tango and Mrs. Marquise," chorused the class. "And thank you!" Dontel and Smashie grinned and waved energetically at their grandmothers.

"You're welcome, Room 11!" said Smashie's grammy.

"It was our pleasure to make your snack," added Mrs. Marquise.

"How kind," Ms. Early said. "Please take a seat."

The child-size chairs in Room 11 made the two women look as though they were kissing their own knees, but they gamely took their places on the periphery of the circle of children.

"And, Room 11," said Ms. Early, smiling, "our third chaperone you already know quite well."

"There's a third chaperone?" asked Cyrus. "You only said two yesterday!"

"This chaperone is very special to our school," Ms. Early began. "In fact—"

But Dontel could not hold himself back. "Is it Mr. Bloom?" he cried hopefully.

"It is!" said Ms. Early.

And once again the door swung open, and there stood Mr. Bloom.

All the children cheered. Mr. Bloom was one of their favorite adults at the Rebecca Lee Crumpler Elementary School. He was head custodian and based his operations in a small trailer off to the side of the main school building. The children loved to be sent there on errands, for Mr. Bloom's three favorite hobbies were pruning bonsai trees, opera, and exploring the possibility of alien life-forms, all of which he was happy to share with the students. Best of all, his interest in aliens had led him on a lifelong study of astronomy, and he and Dontel had had many conversations—since Smashie and Dontel had been in kindergarten, even—about this topic. And now he was going to join them on their field trip and be a guest lecturer for their unit on astronomy as well! It was almost too good to be true.

"Good morning, Mr. Bloom!" the children cried.

"Morning," said the custodian, nodding at them. "Morning, Ms. E., Mrs. T., and Mrs. M."

"Good morning!" the women replied.

"I'm glad to see that everyone remembered to wear blue jeans and their red Rebecca Lee Crumpler Elementary hoodies," said Ms. Early.

"So am I," said Mr. Bloom. "Makes you all easy to identify as members of our group."

"But there's just one more thing before we break for recess," said Ms. Early. "There is someone who has something to share."

"I thought this wasn't going to be a normal meeting with sharing," said Joyce.

"Do we have even time?" asked Tatiana. "If we

have recess and the bus is coming to pick us up right after?"

"We have enough time for this," Ms. Early reassured her.

"Smashie doesn't have more hats, does she?" asked Siggie Higgins.

Smashie scowled at him. But she was not the sharer.

"Actually," said Mrs. Marquise, "I'm the one who is going to share."

Room 11's eyes widened. Never before had an adult shared in morning meeting.

"But it's really something Dontel has been working on," Mrs. Marquise continued. She reached into the large tote bag she was carrying and brought out a cardboard tube that had PLANS written on it in large, green, still-damp-looking letters.

"Grandma! No! You didn't!" Dontel was wide-eyed with shock.

"I did," said Mrs. Marquise calmly. "You've been working on this very hard this past week, and I think it is very much in keeping with the spirit of today's field trip for your class to have a look."

"To start off your unit, too," agreed Smashie's grammy.

"You're in on this, too, Mrs. Tango?" Dontel was unbelieving. But also vehement. "No, Grandma," he said. "Please!"

"What is it?" Jacinda asked.

"Yeah, what is it?" asked Joyce. All of the children were interested.

"Will you at least describe it for the class, Dontel?" asked Ms. Early. "We'd love to hear."

"Describe, nothing," said Mrs. Marquise determinedly. And before Dontel could stop her, she opened the tube and pulled out a piece of paper, rolled up like a scroll.

CHAPTER 3

The Drawing

"Sue, would you please hold the other side?" Mrs. Marquise asked Smashie's grammy. And with a flourish, the two women unrolled the paper and held it high for Room 11 to see.

There was a bit of a silence.

"What is it?" asked Charlene.

Dontel mumbled something.

"Speak up, Dontel," Ms. Early told him.

"It's a technically correct drawing of a space rocket," said Dontel, squirming.

Room 11 gasped in awe.

"Wow," said John. "That is a heck of a drawing."

And it was. Full of arrows and sketches from many points of view, the technically correct drawing of a space rocket was a thing to behold. There were colorful brackets and measurements all over the craft, squares with writing in them, and lines pointing to parts of the rocket as well.

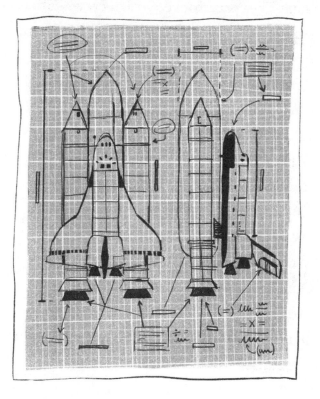

"Grandma," said Dontel plaintively, "why are you embarrassing me?"

"For several reasons. Number one, because I am proud of you."

"No wonder you haven't been able to come over to play that much this week if you've been working on plans for a for-real spaceship!" cried Smashie. "Now it all makes sense! What a great surprise! Is it for a life-size space rocket with a crew?" Smashie was already imagining herself in a Space Rocket Suit, complete with helmet and spongy boots for leaping.

"It's only for a small rocket," mumbled Dontel. "I was just going to make it in my backyard. With you, Smashie."

"Well, I want to see it in real life!" cried Joyce.

"Me too!"

"Same here!"

"What I couldn't do with a rocket like that!" said Billy, rubbing his hands together.

Dontel gave a wordless cry.

Ms. Early quelled Billy with a look.

"I think we have a lot to learn from Dontel's

plans," she said. "We will definitely incorporate it into our unit on space."

"No!" Dontel wailed. "Please, no."

"Why not?" asked Smashie. "It looks great."

"Just wait," Dontel said, and slumped miserably in his spot.

"We can build it in science," said Ms. Early, "and launch it on the athletic fields."

"Ooh!" said Cyrus. "I can't wait to see how far it goes!"

"With no pilot inside?" asked Charlene.

"Just empty?" asked Jacinda.

"Empty, nothing," said Mrs. Marquise. "Dontel left room in the cockpit—"

"Grandma!" Dontel waved his arms to stop her, but it was too late.

"For a special aeronaut," his grandma continued, looking purposefully away from Dontel.

"I'll point," said Grammy helpfully, and she put an explanatory index finger at the nexus of a series of colorful lines that crossed at the seat of the cockpit.

"Who is the pilot?" asked Smashie. But as soon as

she asked, she knew. "Oh," she said. "That's why you didn't want to bring the drawing or the rocket in to school."

"Yes," said Dontel.

"Who?" asked the class. "Who's the pilot?"

"Brnon," mumbled Dontel.

"Who?" asked Mr. Bloom. "Speak up, Mr. M.!"

"The pilot is my Brainyon action figure," said Dontel, raising his head at last. "But I'm not going to let us build my rocket and fire it off if you're going to force me to put my Brainyon action figure inside! We'll just send it up empty."

"Oh, Dontel," pleaded John, who loved Brainyon as much as Smashie and Dontel did. "Please bring in your action figure again? Just to be the pilot that once?"

"Never," said Dontel.

"Aw, come on," said Billy. "I won't do anything. I already got in trouble."

"Exactly," said Dontel, fixing him with a look.

"We can work all that out later," said Ms. Early, holding up a warning hand. "Dontel, suppose you stand by your picture and tell us a bit about how the rocket would work."

"Yes, show us!"

"Please?"

Room 11 was very excited.

Dontel stood reluctantly. "It's sort of like a stomp rocket. Only you just have to push a button. It uses pneumatics."

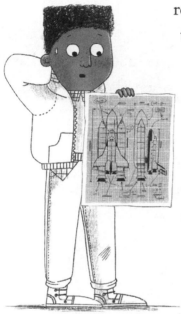

"What does pneumatics mean?" asked John.

"It's a special kind of engineering system that makes use of pressurized air," answered Dontel.

"This is just wonderful!" said Ms. Early. "I am very proud of your work, Dontel."

"I am, too," said Dontel's grandmother.

"So am I," said Smashie's grammy.

"Me too," said Mr. Bloom.

"We all are!" cried Charlene.

"This is especially perfect today," said Ms. Early. "Because"—Ms. Early exchanged smiles with Mrs. Marquise—"I have a wonderful surprise for us. For Dontel, but really, for all of the Rebecca Lee Crumpler Elementary School."

"What is it?"

"Tell us!"

"Well," said Ms. Early, "remember that day last week in morning meeting when the conversation turned to people we look up to?"

"Sure," said Charlene. "I talked about my mom."

"I talked about Mata Hari, international spy!" said Smashie, remembering that lady's smarts, aura of mystery, and glamourous suits.

Dontel rolled his eyes.

"That's right," Ms. Early confirmed. "Who remembers who Dontel discussed?"

"He picked who he always does," said John. "His favorite astrophysicist and the head of the Blayden Planetarium, in New York City, Dr. Cornelius DuVasse Bryson."

"Yes," said Ms. Early. "Well. There just happens to be a meeting of heads of planetariums across the country today at *our* planetarium, and guess who'll be there?"

Dontel blanched. "Not . . . not Dr. Bryson!"

"No, not Dr. Bryson," replied Ms. Early. "But close." She could not contain her smile. "Dr. Bryson's best friend, who is also an astrophysicist!"

"What?!"

"Really?"

"Wow!"

"And not only that," Ms. Early continued, "but there is also a contest running at the planetarium for the best space-related work done by a schoolchild. And guess who is going to be a judge?"

"Not Dr. Bryson's best friend!" Jacinda gasped.

"Exactly Dr. Bryson's best friend!" said Mrs. Marquise.

Ms. Early beamed. "And while we haven't really begun our unit yet and so, unfortunately, have no project to enter as a class, when your grandma called me to tell me about your work on this drawing,

Dontel, I knew your technically correct plans for a rocket would be a perfect entry."

"Yay!"

"Hurrah!"

Room 11 was terribly excited for Dontel. Dontel was also energized, but in a very different way.

"NO!" he cried. He turned away from the class and quickly rolled up the drawing. "I'm not letting this out of my sight until it's done. Otherwise," he continued, glaring at Billy, "it might wind up with a drawing of The Haddock in the cockpit or something."

"Hey!" cried Billy. But he slumped, the light of an idea clearly dying from his eyes.

"That will not happen," said Ms. Early, once again glaring at Billy. "Dontel, please consider letting your grandmother and me enter your drawing in that contest."

"No, thank you," said Dontel. "It's not ready. It's not done! I couldn't have Dr. Bryson's best friend see anything but my most effortful finished work!"

Dontel stuffed the rolled-up drawing furiously but

carefully back in its tube. "This drawing stays private. Pretend you never saw it."

Ms. Early sighed. "Well, the choice is yours," she said. "But I would love it if you would allow me the opportunity to showcase the talents of a Rebecca Lee Crumpler student in that contest."

"And Billy hasn't done anything awful since you brought in your Brainyon and drew your picture," Smashie reminded Dontel.

Dontel looked at her, aghast. "Smashie! Even you? No!"

"I thought you guys forgave me for all my tricks!" said Billy. "I'm funny! I really am!"

"He kind of is, you guys," said Siggie.

"You would say that," said John.

"Children," said Ms. Early, "let's not argue. And Willette Williams and Joyce Costa, stop whispering."

Willette and Joyce leaned away from each other guiltily.

"I'm not arguing," said Dontel. His grandmother sighed and reached for the tube.

"I'll put it back in my tote," she said. "I'm sorry,

Dontel, but this work was too exciting not to share."

But Dontel twitched the tube away from her grasping hand. "*I'll* keep it," he said. "I'll put it in my own backpack right now."

And he went to the back of the room to put his drawing carefully away in his backpack.

"Well," Ms. Early said quietly to Mrs. Marquise, "that flopped."

"Like a haddock," Mrs. Marquise replied, and neither woman could help laughing.

But then Ms. Early sighed. "Children," she said, "I think it's time you all went outside for recess."

"Yes," said Grammy. "Get your yayas out. So there's less wiggling on the long, long bus ride."

"Ugh for long bus rides," said Billy, and there were murmurs of agreement.

"But yay for planetariums at the end of them!" shouted Joyce and the class agreed with gusto. There were shouts of "Yay!" all about the room.

"Exactly," said Ms. Early. "Line up, Room 11."

"Ms. Early," said Smashie slowly, "may I please wash my hands before we go outside?"

"How'd they get so dirty?" Grammy asked. "You've barely been in school fifteen minutes."

"I fell outside before the bell rang." *While practicing my spying.* But Smashie didn't say that part out loud.

"Of course you may wash your hands," said Ms. Early.

Smashie threaded her way to the back of the room. But although she headed for the area with the sink and cubbies, Smashie had no intention of merely washing her hands. For she had a plan.

CHAPTER 4

Smashie's Plan

Carefully, Smashie turned on the taps of the sink. Under the cover of the running water, she glanced over her shoulder and saw that Dontel was deep in conversation with John.

Good, thought Smashie grimly. Then she turned her attention to the pile of backpacks next to the cubbies. There was Dontel's black Brainyon backpack. And next to it was Smashie's own black Brainyon backpack. The only difference between the two was that Smashie's bulged with her somewhat disorganized possessions. But it was not her own backpack

Smashie reached for in the pile of backpacks right now. It was Dontel's.

Quickly and quietly, Smashie unzipped Dontel's backpack and pulled out the tube containing his technically correct drawing of a space rocket, making sure her back was to the children lining up for recess. And then she put Dontel's tube into her own backpack and zipped it firmly.

Smashie was breathing rather hard. After all, she had just stolen her best friend's private property.

But it's for the greater good, she thought firmly. *I am going to break rules three, four, and five and sneak away during the planetarium show, when the room is darkened, and find Dr. Cornelius DuVasse Bryson's best friend to give Dontel's drawing to!*

For that was Smashie's plan. She would also give Dr. Bryson's best friend a slip of paper with the address of the Rebecca Lee Crumpler Elementary School on it so the tube could be mailed back with a letter of praise about Dontel's work and then Room 11 could make the rocket in science class. The whole thing would take about four days, Smashie figured. One for Dr. Bryson's best friend to look at the technically correct picture of the space rocket, and three for it to come back to the school via the US Postal Service with Dr. Bryson's best friend's—or even Dr. Bryson's!—letter of praise. *A wonderful reward for Dontel's work,* Smashie thought. Plus four days was plenty of time for Room 11 to learn a little astronomy before they built that rocket. And build it they would. Smashie would make sure of that.

I hate to lie to my own best friend, thought Smashie, *but if he discovers that his technically correct drawing of a space rocket is not in his backpack, I am just going to say that he must have put it in his cubby instead. That drawing deserves to be seen by Dr. Bryson's best friend!*

And, finally, after giving her hands a cursory wash, Smashie ran to join her class in line to go out for recess.

CHAPTER 5

Gone!

But before the class could leave the room for recess, Mr. Bloom clapped his hand to his forehead.

"Wait a minute now, Ms. E.!" he said. "I plumb forgot to bring over all those books and resources you wanted for this unit."

"We can get them when we come back," Ms. Early reassured Mr. Bloom. "We wouldn't have time to look at them today, anyway."

"Oh, please can we get them now?" asked Willette.

"It would be so cool to come back to Room 11 tomorrow and already have space stuff to look at."

"Let me go get them!"

"Let me!"

As usual, everyone clamored to be allowed to go with Mr. Bloom to his trailer.

"Let Dontel go," said Joyce unexpectedly. "He likes astronomy the best out of everyone."

"Heck, I like it, too," said Billy.

"Only when you draw on people's drawings of Brainyon in a space suit," said Dontel.

Billy threw up his hands.

"Joyce is right," said Willette, exchanging nods with her. "Smashie, you go, too. You guys are kind of the bosses of space right now."

"By the time this unit is done, we'll all be the bosses of space," said Dontel. "Are you all sure?"

There were mutters of "I like astronomy, too" from Tatiana and "Is that fair?" from John, who reminded the class that he'd gone to space camp last summer. But there were also murmurs of "That's true" and "They have been" until all the other volunteering children slowly put their hands down.

"Why, how kind, Room 11," said Ms. Early. "Are you sure?"

"Sure we're sure," said Joyce. "We'll have our turns going the next bunch of times."

"Yay!" said Smashie. "And don't worry, Ms. Early. We can get our yayas out on the way to Mr. Bloom's trailer."

Their grandmothers exchanged glances but said not a word as they headed toward the teachers' lounge with Ms. Early.

"Gde zhe ty, moi zhelennyi?" a lady sang Russianly from the open door of Mr. Bloom's trailer. Since he was such an opera fan, opera ladies could be heard from Mr. Bloom's trailer for most of the day. But when they entered the trailer, Mr. Bloom snapped the music player off.

"Good thing I came back," he said. "Wouldn't want to have wasted the electric. Now here's some boxes of stuff for Room 11. Pick 'em up careful like. Bend from the knees and hoist. Don't want you throwing out your back. I'll carry the real heavy ones."

"Are you excited to be our guest lecturer, Mr. Bloom?" asked Smashie.

"Sure am," replied Mr. Bloom, puffing somewhat as they left the trailer and headed back toward the main building, the heavy boxes in his arms. "Why, it's a pleasure to share what I love with you young ones. Especially when you're so excited to learn!"

"Our class is mostly always pretty excited to learn," said Dontel.

"Except for handwriting," said Smashie.

"That's just you," said Dontel, and Smashie scowled at him.

"I do my best," she said. "I can't help it if my handwriting is messy."

Dontel opened his mouth, but Mr. Bloom was already talking.

"What's this space-related snack I hear your grandmothers brought in for us to eat on the way to the planetarium?"

Dontel and Smashie exchanged looks. The snack was supposed to be a surprise, but after all, it was Mr. Bloom who was asking, and who would appreciate the space-related snack more than Mr. Bloom?

"It's cookies," said Smashie finally. "Special ones. Beautiful ones."

"Sugar cookies with frosting designs of stars and supernovas and galaxies on them," Dontel confided.

"Sounds delicious," said Mr. Bloom, puffing a bit under the weight of his boxes. "How'd they make the stars?"

"Little dots of white icing. We helped," said Smashie. It had been glorious, not only to bake the cookies but to imagine herself into the galaxies they had painted on them. What if she lived on a planet full of methane gas and everything looked orange? Or what if she stepped on a planet with so little gravity that she had to take huge leaps to go wherever she went? Or what if she could navigate a spacecraft from world to world until she met all the kinds of beings that were on them in the whole galaxy? Smashie wriggled with happiness at the remembrance of her imaginings.

"Well, now, some of those dots might not be stars at all. They might be galaxies themselves," said Mr. Bloom. "Can't tell them apart from stars with the naked eye. Heck, you'd need the Hubble telescope most of the time to really see a whole galaxy."

"What's the Hubble telescope?" asked Smashie.

"It's one of the largest telescopes in the world," said Dontel. "It's been launched out in space for years now, taking pictures and sending information back to Earth."

"Oh," said Smashie. "Wow."

"The pictures it sends are beautiful," Dontel continued. "Supernovas, galaxies, everything."

"We made supernovas on some of the other cookies by painting bursty icing on them in clouds, Mr. Bloom!" said Smashie.

"And we made the Andromeda galaxy on some with the spirals all swirly," said Dontel.

"Nice," said Mr. Bloom as they neared the entrance to the school. "By the way, Mr. M., that rocket drawing you did is first-rate."

"No, it isn't," said Dontel. "Not yet. You probably couldn't see from where you were sitting in our meeting circle, but there are still a few things I need to add."

"Nonsense," said Mr. Bloom. "Your grandma came by to show it to me while we were waiting for you kids to start morning meeting."

"She showed it to you up close? Without telling me?" Dontel was disbelieving.

"Yep," said Mr. Bloom. "I went over it with a fine-tooth comb, and it really is technically correct. That rocket, the way you designed it, would work for anybody."

"That's wonderful!" cried Smashie. "Dontel, slap our hands with your hand!"

Dontel slapped both of his friends' hands with his hand, but Smashie could tell he was still troubled. "It still needs a little work," he said. "I was going to show it to you when it was all the way done, Mr. Bloom. In private. With Smashie," he added hastily.

"I think it's all done right now, young man," said Mr. Bloom. "What else could it need?"

But Smashie knew. Dontel needed Brainyon to be in its cockpit. The rocket could never feel complete without that hero at its helm, eyes staring straight into space and steering that rocket with the power of the gadgets he had created. And with Billy on the loose, there was no way to be sure nothing awful would happen, both to the rocket and the action figure.

The trio reached the door of Room 11 just as Miss Martone's whistle sounded on the playground, signaling the end of recess.

"That was quick," said Smashie, surprised.

"She's mad at us," said Billy, overhearing her as Room 11 came boiling back into the room. "John and Joyce both had to come back inside for things they forgot, and Miss Martone got sick of it." He grinned. "At least it wasn't my fault." For indeed, more than once, Room 11 had been sent in because of Billy's bad behavior. Once he had tied all the jump ropes together in knots. Another time, he had released all of the basketballs at once so they tumbled across the blacktop and people fell. And yet a third time, he had raced through a tag game, bopping people on the shoulder until everybody thought they'd been tagged out and the game was ruined.

Billy really could be kind of terrible sometimes.

But Charlene said, "It doesn't matter that Miss Martone sent us in—because look! The field-trip bus is here to take us to the planetarium!"

And Room 11 erupted in cheers as everyone looked out the window and saw the little yellow bus.

"Just one thing," said Smashie's grammy in a puzzled voice. "I don't see Mrs. Marquise's tote bag that we brought the surprise space-related snack in. I could swear we left it right here by the door when we all went out. Has anyone seen it?"

"No!"

"Not me!"

"Oh, no!"

"Not again!"

"Something we need is always going missing!"

"Now, children," said Ms. Early, "let's not get silly. Let's just get to work finding that tote bag. Quickly now." She clapped her hands.

Room 11 looked and looked.

Siggie looked in the reading corner. "Nothing here," he said.

"Same here," said Willette from the meeting area.

"AHOY THE HADDOCK!" A cry sounded from the back of the room by the cubbies. It was Billy, of course. "I FOUND THE TOTE BAG! IT'S HERE!"

"Phew," said Grammy. "This is a long day, and you all would be hungry without a space-related snack to tide you over."

"Phew, nothing," said Dontel's grandmother, taking the bag Billy handed her. "This tote is empty. The plastic container with the space-related snacks inside is gone!"

CHAPTER 6

Billy in Trouble

Room 11 erupted.

"Billy," said John, "fork them over."

"It wasn't me! You just think so because Dontel reminded you at morning meeting what I did to his Brainyon drawing and action figure the other week!"

"That's right," said Joyce. "So do like John says and fork those snacks over right now."

"I don't have them, I tell you!"

"Well, regardless, I'm afraid we have to leave right

now." Ms. Early's voice was stern. "I will say if this is a joke perpetrated by a member of Room 11, I don't think it's a very funny one. And I won't let it spoil our day. But if I find out who took those space-related snacks, that person will not enjoy our trip for long."

"We spent a lot of time baking that snack!" Smashie and Dontel were furious as the sea of their red-hoodied, blue-jeaned classmates lined up to get name tags from the chaperones before they got on the bus.

"That's true!" said Mrs. Marquise. "And to think that a member of this very class may have stolen it! Who'd have thought?"

Smashie's grammy shook her head in disappointed agreement.

"Don't worry, Mrs. Marquise!" cried Smashie. "Dontel and I will find out who took our snack if it's the last thing we do!"

"Yay!" cried Charlene. "You two are excellent investigators. Now you can investigate the mystery of where the space-related snack went. We all want a snack!"

"Yeah!"

"We love snacks!"

"Don't you worry," Dontel reassured Room 11. "Investigating is exactly what we'll do."

"Good-bye, Patches!" called Willette to the little hamster in the back of the room as they left. "We will see you when our families come to pick us up late this afternoon!"

But little did they know that, well before they returned to their families at the end of the day, Room 11 would be rocked by a trio of robberies that would shake them to their cores. Indeed, if attention had been paid as to who was going where when on that long, long bus ride and in the planetarium, the robberies might have been prevented from the start. But attention was not paid. And thus, the crimes— and the investigations—would unfold.

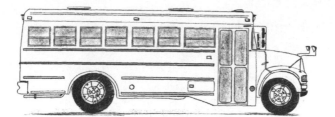

CHAPTER 7
GONE!

Smashie and Dontel were the last students to get on the bus. Their usual seat in the back was taken. In fact, all the seats were taken except for one that never was, right in the middle of the bus.

"Rats," said Smashie as they sat down.

"It'll be okay, Smash," said Dontel, who knew Smashie liked to sit farther back, where it was more difficult for Mr. Potter, the bus driver, to keep an eye on her in his mirror.

The two grandmothers were already in the seat opposite them.

"Oh, no!" whispered Smashie. "They will keep an eye on us, too!"

"Well, there won't be much to keep an eye on," said Dontel. "We'll just be sitting on the bus."

"But, Dontel, if we are going to investigate the missing space-related snack, I need to make a Cookie-Investigating Suit!" cried Smashie. "And Mr. Potter is not going to like me moving around to get materials for a suit one bit. Neither are our grandmothers!"

"We aren't allowed to move around when the bus is moving, anyway."

"But the bus isn't moving yet," said Smashie.

It was true. The children and their chaperones were ready to go, but the bus remained parked in front of the Rebecca Lee Crumpler Elementary School. And soon Smashie and Dontel saw why.

"Mr. Potter?" Willette was standing up beside the bus driver's seat. "I don't have my backpack! May I go back in the building and get it?"

Mr. Potter sighed and opened the door of the bus. "Be quick about it. Anybody else forget something?"

And he glanced meaningfully at Smashie in his mirror. Smashie scowled but stopped almost immediately. Mr. Potter did have to wait for her sometimes. He did not deserve a scowl.

"This is great," she said to Dontel. "Waiting for Willette gives me time to make a suit. I am going to consult with Grammy."

Dontel pinched the bridge of his nose and sighed. He himself never wore suits, but Smashie knew that, even if he felt silly about them, he understood how important they were to her.

"Grammy," said Smashie, leaning across Dontel to speak to her grandmother, "Dontel and I are going to investigate the missing space-related snack, so I need to make a suit, quick. What do you think?"

"What about one of the hats you brought in yesterday? I noticed you didn't put them back where they belonged."

"I didn't," Smashie admitted. "But that's a good idea. Which one? That big Russian one? It seems like a good one for having big thoughts in."

"I think the homburg," said Grammy. "More like something a gumshoe would wear. And besides, that

one is fully yours. I went to all the trouble to embroider your—"

"GRAMMY." Smashie tried to quell her grandmother with a look without being disrespectful.
"You know our agreement!"

"I certainly do," said Grammy with a sigh.

"Yes, indeed," said Mrs. Marquise, who was sitting
beside Grammy. "Though why you don't want anyone to know what a pretty name—"

Smashie couldn't scowl at Mrs. Marquise, so she
settled for a "Please, Mrs. Marquise!" with a pleading
look, and that did the trick. Mrs. Marquise fell silent,
shaking her head.

"I am not wearing that homburg," said Smashie.
"Not if it's going to—bring all that up. I should never
have brought it to school in the first place."

"Which one will you wear, then?" asked Grammy.

"The red turban," said Smashie. "It is glamorous,
and people will think I am wearing it to match our
Rebecca Lee Crumpler hoodies."

And she leaned back in her seat.

"All set?" asked Dontel.

"Yes," said Smashie. "I think being in a nearly

all-red Investigator Suit will help me think extra hard." And, backpack on her lap, she reached in for the turban. *I better be careful,* she thought. *Dontel's tube is right on top of my belongings. I should carefully smoosh it to the bottom of my backpack so he won't see it when I am pulling out the turban!*

Smashie put her hand in her backpack. There was the fur of the Russian helmet and the silky fabric of the turban, but where was Dontel's tube?

This is what I get for being so messy, she thought. Her questioning hand dove to the very bottom of the backpack. Her pencils, papers, and hats were all there, but something else was not.

The tube with Dontel's technically correct drawing of the rocket was missing.

CHAPTER 8

Smashie Panics

Before Smashie could think another thought, Mr. Potter threw the bus into gear and they were off. Smashie's face grew hot with shock and worry. She pulled out the large red satin turban and put it on, her mind working like sixty. Could she have put the tube in Dontel's identical Brainyon backpack by mistake? But, no, that made no sense! Why would she take it out of his backpack and put it right back in? Besides—the nest of papers, the hats—she knew the backpack she had put the tube in had been hers.

"Why are you so red?" asked Dontel. "Do you feel dumb in your hat?"

"No," said Smashie. "I love my turban. And everyone else will, too." But inside, her brain felt like Patches the hamster running on his wheel.

What had happened to that tube?

CHAPTER 9

Diverting Attention

Now there were *two* mysteries to solve. It was all terribly confusing. And terribly terrible.

Smashie fished about in her backpack some more and pulled out two small notebooks. One of the notebooks said FIRST STREET BAPTIST on the cover, while the other featured a thoughtful-looking horse.

"Our Investigation Notebooks!" Dontel cried. "I didn't know you had them with you!"

"I always carry them now," said Smashie. "What

with all these mysteries popping up for us to investigate. And lucky thing I have them today." *Boy, is it,* she thought. *Now that I have to investigate Dontel's missing tube as well!*

"I'll get us pencils," Dontel said, and made to reach into his own backpack, which, Smashie knew, was neat as a pin, like his room and desk at school.

"Don't worry," Smashie said hastily. "I have pencils."

But it was too late. Now it was Dontel's face that gave away his feelings. He blanched.

"Smashie," said Dontel desperately, "the tube with my technically correct picture of the space rocket is not in my backpack! It's gone!"

"Oh, nonsense," said Smashie airily, aware her face was still a hot and fiery red. At least she had made a plan for this moment. "I think you must have stuck it in your cubby instead of your backpack," she said. "Safer that way. All this traveling and all." Smashie stumbled over her words. She was not used to lying to her best friend. And to be lying *and* responsible for losing his drawing—it was all too much to bear. What was she going to do?

Dontel pierced her with a look.

"Why are you piercing me with a look?" Smashie cried. "You are a logical person. And you probably thought that it would be more logical to leave the drawing at school safely in your cubby than risk it getting all banged up on this bumpy bus trip."

The ride certainly was bumpy. But Smashie's face burned hotter than ever.

Dontel shook his head. "You are just trying to make me feel better," he said. "I would never have put it in my cubby. Too easy for my grandma to take out. Or worse, for Billy to get his hands on! Plus, I very clearly remember putting the tube in my backpack. And now it's gone!" He gulped with unhappiness and upset. "Smashie, someone must have taken my technically correct drawing of a space rocket!"

"Maybe it just fell out of your backpack," said Smashie rather desperately. "Things fall out of my backpack all the time." *Was that it? Had Dontel's tube fallen out of her messy backpack?* But even Smashie, as messy as she could be with her belongings, didn't believe this. She had been very careful with that tube.

"Let's get back to investigating the missing space-related snack," Smashie said now, as firmly as she could, given her guilt. For she had stolen and then somehow lost her best friend's most complex project to date. And there was no one to blame but herself for that betrayal.

CHAPTER 10

Double Investigation

"Forget the mystery of the missing space-related snack!" Dontel cried. "We have to investigate the disappearance of my drawing right now! I've been working on it for a *week*! I researched and everything!"

Smashie had never seen her friend look quite so upset.

Apparently, she looked the same way to Dontel.

"Smashie," he said, "I've never seen you look quite so upset. It is awfully nice of you to be worried about my missing drawing, too."

"Thank you," said Smashie hurriedly. "But shouldn't we investigate the missing space-related snack first?" That might give her time to think of a plan to find that drawing!

Dontel look startled and betrayed. "Smashie," he said, "don't you think my drawing is more important than cookies?"

And, although Smashie thought few things were as important as cookies, she had to admit Dontel was right.

"You are right," she agreed.

"Then let me have my notebook, please," said Dontel. "And you better fix that turban."

The turban was sloshing a bit rakishly over one of Smashie's eyes. "This turban is from the 1920s," she explained. "And sized for an adult. All this bumping on the bus is making it go crooked." And she tossed her head back to center the turban above her face once again.

Maybe they should *investigate the missing drawing instead of the space-related snack,* thought Smashie as she pulled her ears out from under the turban to make it stay on better. Teaming up with Dontel would make her feel more confident that the drawing might be found. After all, she knew firsthand what a wonderful investigator Dontel was. Even if she would need to conceal from him how the drawing had originally disappeared.

That would be Too Much, thought Smashie. And besides, she knew her plan for giving his drawing to Dr. Bryson's best friend would certainly make Dontel angry. Look how mad he had been at his own grandma! And even their beloved Ms. Early! Maybe he would think Smashie had betrayed him, too, and not even want to be her best friend anymore!

Smashie's stomach sank.

"I'm starving!" moaned Joyce from her seat two rows behind them, at the back of the bus. "I sure wish we could have our space-related snack!"

"Me too!"

"I'm so hungry!"

"Well, children, I am sorry about that," said Ms. Early. "But you know I can't help you. And Smashie and Dontel and their grandmothers worked hard on that snack, too." It was clear Ms. Early was still disappointed with the snack swiper.

"Smashie and Dontel," said Willette from her seat next to Siggie behind them. "You are both excellent investigators." Her voice hardened briefly. "For the most part."

Siggie nudged her, and Willette's voice softened: "Anyway, you are good at finding lost things and figuring things out. Can't you solve this mystery for us?"

Dontel and Smashie looked at each other gravely. Of course the space-related snack was important. But Dontel's drawing was more so. Should they tell the kids the rocket plans were missing? Smashie spoke the question to Dontel with her eyes. He shook his head vehemently.

"No!" he whispered fiercely. "I don't want anyone to know! What if Billy finds it and draws The Haddock in the cockpit before I can get it back? If he doesn't have it already," he said darkly.

"Don't get ahead of ourselves," Smashie whispered back. Swiveling to look back at Willette and Siggie, she called, "We will be happy to investigate. But we have some, uh, work to do first."

"What's this work you have to do first? Are you two putting off the investigation?"

It was Grammy, aghast.

"If the children have work to do, why don't *we* investigate the missing space-related snack?" suggested Dontel's grandma. "We baked it—"

"With our help!" cried Smashie indignantly.

"Yes," said Grammy. "But Lorraine and I can surely be the ones who detect where it is!" Smashie knew Grammy's confidence in investigating was borne from the two grandmothers' love of mystery stories. They had read their way steadily through the mystery section at the library and were members of a detective book club that met every other week to discuss mysteries and forensic methodology.

The grandmothers were terribly excited.

"But—but," sputtered Alonso from his seat behind Ms. Early, "Smashie and Dontel always solve our mysteries."

"We don't want them to feel excluded," said Cyrus.

"Oh," said Mrs. Tango, and her shoulders wilted.

"We don't feel excluded!" cried Smashie, who in fact felt wonderfully relieved about the whole thing. If their grandmothers investigated the cookies, she and Dontel would be free to investigate the missing drawing!

"How about both teams of detectives detect the missing space-related snack?" suggested Dontel.

"Dontel," whispered Smashie fiercely, "what are you doing? I thought you thought there was no way cookies were more important than your drawing?"

"Cookies are always important," whispered Dontel back. "But I have a plan. We can investigate the missing drawing *under the cover of investigating the mystery of the missing space-related snack.*"

"Great idea!" Smashie whispered, and beamed. She called over to the grandmothers, "Better get ready or we'll solve the case before you!"

"Don't be too sure about that!" said Mrs. Marquise. And the two ladies bent their heads together in earnest conversation.

"I think we should tackle this the same way we did our other cases," Dontel said, once everyone on the bus had stopped looking at the two of them.

"We have to think about motive—*why* someone would commit the crime—as well as opportunity—the chance to take my technically correct drawing of a space rocket. And those will lead us to suspects." Dontel opened to a fresh page in his notebook. Smashie did the same.

"Ooh, *motive, opportunity,* and *suspects!* Three of my favorite investigator words!" For in the back of their Investigation Notebooks, the two investigators kept a page of Investigator Language, which they consulted regularly and added to often. "I wish I had that sash I made with pockets sewn on to hold clues," Smashie said wistfully. "At least this is one time when we don't have to hide that we are investigating from the kids."

"Yes," said Dontel. "But you are already in a suit, Smash, and if a kid does mind that we are investigating, why, then they are probably a suspect, because they don't want to be discovered!"

Smashie squirmed in her turban. She certainly did not want to be discovered, though she knew that Dontel was not thinking of her.

At the top of clean pages in their notebooks, they wrote:

THE MISSING TECHNICALLY CORRECT
DRAWING OF A SPACE ROCKET

"Let's start with motive," said Dontel. They were still speaking in low tones so the children in the seats around them wouldn't hear their true investigation. "What would make someone want my technically correct drawing of a rocket?"

"I can think of a billion motives," said Smashie, relieved that Dontel's mind was diverted from suspects, at least for the moment. Besides, Smashie could always think of a billion reasons why people would want to commit the crimes she and Dontel investigated. "Maybe it was an alien who was spying on you from outer space and saw you were onto something! Maybe it was

important people in the govern-
ment who are afraid you will get
to another planet before they
do! Maybe it was a mad rocket
scientist who has been trying for
years to make a working rocket
and is jealous of your success!"
Smashie's eyes were flashing.

"Or maybe it's someone who
wants to put The Haddock in
the cockpit and name it The Haddock Fish-Ship,"
said Dontel darkly.

"You really think it is Billy this time, don't you?"
said Smashie.

"He's had it in for me ever since
he got in so much trouble for swiping my Brainyon action figure the
other week!"

"But to wreck your plans—that
would be super mean, even for
Billy."

"He wrecked my drawing that

day," Dontel reminded Smashie once again. "Billy doesn't always know the line."

Smashie had to admit this was true.

"Maybe the motive is someone wanted to take it for safekeeping from Billy, then," said Smashie. "They took it out of your backpack"—she gulped—"and put it somewhere Billy couldn't guess so he couldn't ruin it with a picture of The Haddock."

But who knew it was in my backpack? thought Smashie.

It was very hard to think along two parallel lines of investigating at once.

"Or maybe it was someone jealous that you did such a good job on the rocket drawing," she said aloud. "Someone who could never do it themselves."

"People aren't usually jealous in Room 11," Dontel pointed out.

"Sometimes we are," said Smashie. "I am jealous of all the athletic people."

"You could be athletic if you tried to be, Smash," said Dontel.

"No, I couldn't. I hate when people hit balls at

me at high speed. And I am a slow runner. I'd rather just watch." She thought. "Actually, if I were to be granted a wish by a magical wizard, I think I might wish to be super amazing at a sport and have all of Room 11 want me on their team." She sighed. "Anyway, the point is, people do get jealous sometimes, and maybe someone got jealous of the attention you got for your rocket smarts."

"I feel dumb putting that down."

"But we really should write everything down. Even the ones about aliens and mad scientists." Smashie did love a mad scientist.

"I have one more idea," she continued, her palms sweating a bit with worry that Dontel might guess her own motive for stealing his drawing. "It could be someone who thought the drawing was beautiful and wanted to hang it up in their own home."

"It wasn't that beautiful," said Dontel, modestly hanging his head.

"It was!" Smashie cried. "All those colors of ink! All those lines and shapes and points of view! It was just super!"

"Maybe you took it, then, if you thought it was so nice," Dontel joked.

Smashie's mouth fell open.

"Hey, I'm just kidding," said Dontel.

"I know," said Smashie, trying to keep the panic out of her voice. But her face grew hot once more.

"WHO LIKES COOKIES?" boomed a voice from beside them. Everybody jumped. It was Grammy, clearly getting on with motives herself, in the grandmothers' space-related snack investigation.

Slowly, hands raised all over the bus. "Is that what the space-related snack was, Mrs. Marquise and Mrs. Tango?" asked Charlene.

"Yes," said Mrs. Marquise. "Though we may have investigated the question more discreetly." She looked over her glasses at Grammy.

"Discreet, nothing," said Grammy. "We have to get to the bottom of this. They can't have another theft in Room 11! Why, these children have already been through the wringer this year!"

"But Smashie and Dontel have solved all our mysteries," said Cyrus.

"I don't care who solves what mystery," said Mr. Potter wearily, "as long as no kids move around on my bus." He glanced at Smashie in the mirror.

"That's right," Ms. Early reiterated.

"I'm not moving!" Smashie protested. "I am sitting very nicely in my seat!"

"Detecting those cookies, I hope," said John, who was sitting with Cyrus in the seat in front of Smashie and Dontel.

"Yes," Smashie lied. Her mind was spinning. Even if they found the tube, how would she be able to snatch it away again to give to Dr. Bryson's best friend? What a mess! She had tried to fix a problem to overcome Dontel's modesty and shyness and now here she was, having to fix her fix-it. The family's fatal flaw, Grammy always said. It came from being hasty.

This time it didn't, though, thought Smashie. *This time I was careful. Or so I thought!*

"Let's move on to opportunity," said Dontel, and they wrote Opportunity in large letters on the next page of their notebooks.

"Well," said Smashie, "everybody had opportunity

when the class was looking for the space-related snack."

"Let's write that down," said Dontel. "But that also rules out some kids right away. Like Siggie was checking in the reading corner. Willette was in the meeting area. They couldn't have been looking so hard for the cookies and also gotten back to the cubbies and backpack area in time to steal my drawing."

"True enough, "said Smashie. "Shall we start a Suspects List and cross them out?"

"Yes," said Dontel firmly.

Smashie wrote that down and underneath:

1. ~~Siggie~~
2. ~~Willette~~

"And *we* were looking in the science corner," said Smashie carefully. "So we can rule ourselves out. Ha-ha!" Her laugh was weak.

Dontel looked at her as if she were daft. "Well, of course," he said. "But that doesn't even bear writing down, does it?"

"Of course not," said Smashie hurriedly. "I was just joking around."

Dontel looked at her strangely.

"Do we have any other suspects to put on the list?" Smashie asked, hoping to distract him once more.

"Billy," said Dontel firmly.

"I really don't think so, Dontel," said Smashie. "I think you are just mad."

"We are putting him on the list," said Dontel, and reluctantly, Smashie joined him in adding:

3. Billy

And as the first item on the Motives List, they wrote:

1. Revenge for getting in trouble about Brainyon

"Who else?" Dontel tapped his teeth with his pencil.

Smashie fidgeted uncomfortably.

"What's the matter, Smash? Why are you so fidgety?"

Smashie forced herself to be still.

"I am just worried about your drawing," she said, happy to say an honest thing at last.

"Thank you, Smash," said Dontel. "I really appreciate that sentiment."

"I want a cookie!" It was Billy, from his seat in front of Mr. Bloom at the back of the bus. "Where is our space-related snack?"

"Yeah!" cried Tatiana from her seat up front, across from Ms. Early. "Dontel and Smashie, do you have any leads yet?"

"Don't you all worry," called Mrs. Marquise. "Mrs. Tango and I are also working the case."

"'Working the case!'" Smashie and Dontel said in unison. What a wonderful way to say "investigating"!

"Let's add that phrase to our Investigator Language page," said Dontel. And they did.

Smashie looked across the aisle at the investigating grandmothers. Her grammy had even gotten out her needlepoint. She had just taken up the hobby, but she said it helped her think. Right now she was working on a geometric design full of polygons. "I have to do a pattern with all straight lines," she said to Dontel's grandma now. Jacinda, sitting next to Billy behind the two chaperones, looked interestedly at Grammy's hoop over the seat back. "I can't embroider curved lines yet, and I surely couldn't concentrate on that missing space-related snack if I tried to learn now."

And she and Mrs. Marquise chuckled. But soon their voices grew low and serious.

In front of Smashie and Dontel, John and Cyrus exchanged concerned looks. *Clearly,* thought Smashie, *they were not yet convinced of the grandmothers' investigating skills.*

CHAPTER 11

Investigating!

"Speaking of those cookies," boomed another voice from the back of the bus. It was Mr. Bloom, who was seated in the very back seat to keep an eye on the children there. "Speaking of those cookies, did you know that some of them were decorated with frosting images of the Andromeda galaxy? Complete with its swirling arms?"

"How did you know about that?" called Grammy back to Mr. Bloom.

"Yes, how?" said Mrs. Marquise. "The decorations were meant to be a surprise." And the two grandmothers gave Smashie and Dontel a hard look.

Dontel and Smashie exchanged guilty looks. "We told Mr. Bloom about the decorations," Smashie confessed. "We figured it was all right because he is an adult and our guest lecturer."

"Hrmm," said the grandmothers.

"Forget that!" cried a startled Billy. "Galaxies have *arms*?"

"Yes," said Mr. Bloom. "Some galaxies have arms full of stars that spiral around in a big galactic swirl."

"Phew," said Billy. "I thought you meant like galactic tentacles reaching out to grab us." And he waved his arms tentacly about.

All the children laughed. Except Dontel.

"You won't be laughing in billions of years," he called back to where Billy was sitting. "When our galaxies collide and those arms tentacle out and grab our galaxy, the Milky Way, just like that."

Billy gulped.

"Don't worry, son," said Mr. Bloom. "That's a long ways away."

"That was kind of mean, Dontel," said Smashie, who, as a budding thief herself, was a fine one to talk.

Dontel shrugged. "I think Billy deserves to worry a little," he said.

Smashie said nothing.

"Let's work on our Opportunity List," said Dontel now. "And make it methodical."

"Okay," said Smashie.

"I've been thinking it had to be someone who had cause to be near the cubbies and the pile of backpacks," said Dontel.

"Let's write that down," said Smashie, though her stomach began to churn.

So under the word Opportunity on a new page of their notebooks, they wrote:

1. Had to be someone who had cause to be near the cubbies and the pile of backpacks

"That is sort of all of Room 11, but not really," said Dontel. "We've already talked about the class wandering around looking for our space-related snack. Let's see, though. Who specially had cause to be in the back of the room?"

"Well," said Smashie, feeling terrible to throw a classmate under the bus, "Cyrus was Hamster Monitor this morning. He had to be by the cubbies to feed Patches."

"Great thinking, Smashie! We can add Cyrus to the Suspects List and *Feeding Patches* to the Opportunity List."

"Did you say my name?" Cyrus's head swiveled around from the seat in front of them.

"Um, yes?" said Smashie unhappily.

"Am I a suspect?" Cyrus almost seemed happy to be considered one. He was such a nice boy. It probably felt good to him to be seen as a little bad sometimes.

"I do like cookies." Cyrus laughed and swiveled his head back around to John, who laughed with him.

"What about knowledge of which backpack is mine?" Dontel asked now.

"That should be item three on the list," agreed Smashie. And they wrote:

3. Knowledge of which backpack is Dontel's

"Though everybody knows you have a black Brainyon backpack," Smashie pointed out. "Dontel," she began mendaciously, "maybe the tube fell out of your backpack in the pile and the person put it in your cubby!"

"You and my cubby," Dontel said with a sigh. "In that case, why don't we just shout and ask the people on the bus if they saw the tube with my drawing in it and put it in my cubby? Sure would save me a lot of worry." But his voice clearly showed he did not believe for one minute that someone had taken the tube for kind or tidy reasons.

"We're not allowed to shout on the bus," said Smashie, who knew firsthand from past experience.

"Who else could have been by our cubbies and backpacks?" Dontel tapped his teeth with the pencil once more. "I know! Anyone who had to use the sink!"

Smashie's mind was wild. "John washed the paintbrushes this morning from when some of the kids used them yesterday afternoon during Writers' Workshop to make illustrations for their stories," she said hurriedly, feeling terrible once more to throw a classmate under the bus.

"True," said Dontel, eycing her.

Smashie's stomach churned.

"Let's put that down," he said, and so they added:

4. Access to the sink

to the Opportunity List.
And to the Suspect List, under:

4. Cyrus

they added:

5. John

Dontel eyed her steadily. "Smashie," he said, "you were back by the sink, washing your hands. Did you notice anything?"

"No." Smashie laughed weakly. "If I had, our case would be solved already, right?"

Dontel reached over in the direction of Smashie's pencil. But it wasn't her pencil he wanted.

"What," he asked, "is this smudge on your finger?"

"What smudge?" asked Smashie.

"Right here." Dontel touched the tip of her left index finger. Sure enough, there was a green smudge.

Ink! thought Smashie wildly. "I . . . I don't know," she said weakly. "I must have gotten it on there during Writers' Workshop yesterday."

"But you only used pencil to write your story in Writers' Workshop," said Dontel. "I was with you."

Smashie gulped.

"We always say we have to look at the clues very carefully," said Dontel. "No matter who is incriminated."

Smashie's palms began to sweat afresh.

"When someone is supposed to bc washing their hands, they are certainly back by the sink near the cubbies and backpacks. So: opportunity to be by the sinks and pile of backpacks, check." Dontel's voice was stern. "And when somebody handles a tube that my grandma just wrote the word PLANS on in big letters in green marker before she brought it in to school, they get smudges on their hands. Grandma"—he turned to face his grandmother in the seat opposite—"may I see your hands, please?"

"My hands?" asked Mrs. Marquise. "Why?"

"Can I just please see them?" Dontel asked.

Mrs. Marquise raised her hands in the air, and sure enough, there were some green smudges on her fingers.

"I am making a Clues List," said Dontel. And he did, writing:

CLUES

1. Green smudges on hands

"So," he continued, "incriminating smudge on index finger, also check."

Dontel drew himself up. "Smashie McPerter, I am adding someone to the Suspects List."

And in large letters, he wrote:

6. YOU

CHAPTER 12

The Fight

"Me?!" cried Smashie. This was terrible! Usually she was the one who suspected herself in their cases and Dontel was the one to talk her down. But now Dontel, first-rate investigator, was the one to suspect her—and rightly—and he was first-rately investigating *her*!

"Admit it," Dontel pressed. "You stole my drawing! But why? It's the motive I can't figure out. Did you want to build it yourself without me?" Dontel's voice was incredulous.

"I wish I were a better hand washer," said Smashie miserably, staring at her hands. "I confess, Dontel. But of course I wasn't going to build it without you. I . . . I was going to take it and give it to Dr. Bryson's best friend to look at, along with the address of the Rebecca Lee Crumpler Elementary School so it could be sent back to you with a letter of praise. I was proud of you, Dontel! Your drawing deserves to be seen by the best friend of your idol!"

"Smashie," said Dontel, "I am maybe a little bit grateful you are proud of me, but I am *very mad at you for stealing my drawing*. Give it back right now!"

Smashie stared at her hands once more. Finally, she lifted her head.

"I can't," she said. "It's gone."

"Gone?!" cried Dontel. "What do you mean?"

"I mean . . . I mean . . ." Smashie gulped and blinked back tears. "I mean it's not in my backpack anymore, and I don't know where it went."

Dontel gasped. "Do you mean you *lost* my drawing?"

"No!" cried Smashie. "Well, kind of! But I don't

think I did! I put it very carefully in my backpack, and now it's not there!"

"Are you sure? You keep your backpack so messy! Maybe it's in there amid all your hats and papers!"

Smashie was stung at being called messy, but her heart leaped hopefully. Maybe Dontel was right!

"Let's take everything out of my backpack to be sure!" Smashie cried.

And together, she and Dontel took out handfuls of old school papers. They took out the homburg and the big Russian furry hat. They took out the pretend mustache and all of Smashie's pencils.

The backpack was empty. There was no tube.

"Smashie McPerter, that tears it!" said Dontel. "You're always losing things! Why do you have to be so disorganized? Now my plans are lost and it's all your fault!"

Smashie sat back, shamed. Dontel was saying things that were all the more terrible for being true.

"Well, you are too particular about your backpack," she shot back weakly.

"No, I am not," said Dontel. "I know where my

things are. And I don't take things that belong to other people that they expressly said were not ready to be seen by Dr. Bryson's best friend!"

"Dontel! We can't fight! We really do have to investigate this case now!" She lowered her voice. "That's why I wasn't honest with you. I'm not proud of it. But I guess I thought since we had to investigate it anyway, I could—"

Dontel cut her off: "You lied to me."

Smashie's face was hotter than ever, and tears sprang to her eyes. "I didn't lie!" she cried. "I just didn't tell you the whole story!"

"Same thing," said Dontel. "Same thing, Smashie McPerter! Or SHOULD I CALL YOU—"

"Dontel!" Smashie sat back, eyes wide. "You promised me you'd never tell!"

"Well, I think friendship promises no lying," said Dontel. "And no taking stuff. Do you know how hard I worked on that drawing? Do you know how much it means to me?"

"Yes!" cried Smashie. "It means just as much to me!" Smashie had never felt so awful in her life. Her best friend! Mad at her!

"Ha!" said Dontel scornfully.

"Dontel, please! I still think someone stole your drawing for nefarious purposes like we were saying," she said desperately. "And we have to investigate!"

"No," said Dontel.

"No?" said Smashie, aghast. "What do you mean, no? We have to! We can't give up. Dr. Bryson wouldn't give up. You told us that when you shared your autographed copy of his book. Back when you used to share. You said he—"

"Oh, I'm not giving up," said Dontel. "I am going to investigate."

He turned his head away from Smashie to face the front of the bus.

"It's just that I am going investigate *alone*."

The silence after his sentence was deafening.

Smashie turned her head and looked out the window. Her shame clouded her vision, but nonetheless she could not help noticing a man in a jumpsuit who was stabbing garbage on the side of the road with a pointy stick and putting it in a bag. He had a big ruff of curly hair and somehow looked familiar to her.

Smashie figured he was being punished for

something. She felt so bad about what had happened that she had the urge to go out and join him.

The man, who indeed had crossed paths with Room 11 of the Rebecca Lee Crumpler School before, watched the bus pass by and waved his fist at it as it disappeared around a corner. Smashie could see him no more.

CHAPTER 13

Bus in Trouble

"Are you two *quarreling?*" asked Grammy from across the bus aisle.

Dontel was quiet. Smashie nodded.

"Whatever about?" asked Mrs. Marquise. "You two disagree sometimes, but you never fight."

"We are now," said Dontel. "You know what she did? She—"

But all conversation ceased as a terrible clanking, dragging noise began, growing louder and louder by the second.

"What's going on?" gasped Joyce.

"Is our bus going to explode?" cried Siggie.

"No," said Cyrus knowledgeably. "I bet it's just the tailpipe. It probably came loose and is dragging on the pavement." His parents were auto mechanics with a shop just down the street from Smashie's and Dontel's houses, and Cyrus knew a lot about vehicles.

"Yup," said Mr. Potter. "I'm going to have to pull over."

The bus lurched to the right and stopped. The sudden cessation of movement made Smashie's turban fall forward over her eyes. It was just as well. She was teary underneath it, and she didn't know what she was going to do.

CHAPTER 14

More Fighting
and Hats

Mr. Potter opened the door of the bus with the big handle by his steering wheel and hurried outside.

"Excuse me, Lorraine." Grammy stood and crossed over her friend to get to the aisle of the school bus. "I know something about cars. Maybe I can help."

"Me too, Ms. Early?" begged Cyrus. "I help my parents all the time! I know just what to do for a dragging tailpipe!"

"Certainly you can confer with the two adults," said Ms. Early. "But I want you to stay on the side of the bus well away from the road. Only adults go in back of the vehicle."

"Okay," Cyrus said, and made his way eagerly to the door of the bus.

"Oh, no!" cried Joyce from her seat at the back of the bus with Charlene. "What if the bus can't be fixed and we can't go to the planetarium after all?"

"Yes!" said Charlene. "What if our families have to come get us by the side of the road and we never get to see the planetarium show?"

Dontel gulped.

"Ms. Early?" asked Smashie with a quivering voice. "May I help, too, with the tailpipe? I've been practicing dangling, and maybe they could lower me down to look under the bus to see what's—"

Dontel shook his head in disgust. "Ms. Early," he said, "may I please sit with my grandma?"

"You all are making my head spin," said Ms. Early. "First, Smashie, of course you may not dangle down under the bus. Second, children, a dragging tailpipe is not a big problem with a motor vehicle, most times. It's usually just a matter of attaching it with some wire to a metal bracket near the tailpipe. So I think we will be fine in terms of making it to the planetarium. We may be a tad late, but I did leave a cushion of time before our activities and the planetarium show begin."

Everyone on the bus breathed a sigh of relief.

"And, yes, Dontel," Ms. Early finished, "you may get up and sit with your grandmother."

"Thank you," said Dontel. And he collected his belongings in a pointedly neat way, then went across the aisle without so much as a glance at Smashie.

What could she do?

And then it came to her.

Investigate!

If Smashie worked the case herself and found Dontel's drawing and got it back to him, maybe he would forgive her and they could go back to being best friends!

"Why did you want to move seats, Dontel?" asked John. "Do you feel sick?"

"No," said Dontel. "Wait. Make that yes." And he

stood up and faced the small bus full of people. "You all," he said in a loud, clear, voice. "I need your help! I can't find my technically correct drawing of a space rocket!"

"What?" The bus was horrified.

"I know," said Dontel. "So could you all please look around your seats and see if it rolled out of Smashie's messy backpack?"

"Dontel," said his grandmother, "what does Smashie have to do with this? And why are you being so rude about her backpack?"

"BECAUSE SHE STOLE MY TECHNICALLY CORRECT DRAWING OF THE SPACE ROCKET AND PUT IT IN HER BACKPACK AND NOW IT'S GONE!" Dontel shouted.

The bus gasped.

"Smashie!"

"You didn't!"

The children's voices were shocked and dismayed. They all looked at one another and then back at Smashie.

"I did take it," said Smashie tearily. "I wanted to

sneak away from the group at the planetarium to give it to Dr. Bryson's best friend to admire and mail back to Dontel with a letter of praise."

"You took it without telling Dontel?" asked Ms. Early. "And you were planning to leave our group without telling me, breaking rule four on our list of rules for the trip?"

"Yes," Smashie said, and sobbed.

The bus was quiet.

"That was very wrong of you, Smashie," said Ms. Early.

"But her heart was in the right place," said Mrs. Marquise.

Smashie wiped her tears. "Do you really think so, Mrs. Marquise?" she asked.

"I do," said Dontel's grandma.

"Me too," said Charlene. "Sometimes you just have to do stuff in a complicated way."

"Well, I think she should have asked," said Billy from the back of the bus. "But you all never like my ideas anyway. If only The Haddock were here, he could use his fishy superpowers to find that drawing!"

"Which fishy superpower?" asked Jacinda.

"The one where he can whirlpool objects up from nowhere," said Billy.

"Grrr," said Dontel.

"Well, I am going to use my own regular powers," said Smashie. "And I am going to investigate where that drawing went. I'll find it if it's the last thing I do!"

"That's the spirit, Smashie," said Mrs. Marquise.

"Grandma, whose side are you on?" cried Dontel.

"*I'll* investigate that drawing if it's the last thing *I* do."

"Why don't you work together?" said Mrs. Marquise. "That's always gone well for you before."

Both children were silent.

"They won't because they're fighting," said Billy.

"Everybody look for that tube right now," said Ms. Early. And all heads bent as the children poked about under their seats and amid their belongings.

"Not here."

"Here, either."

"We don't see it back here, Ms. Early!"

Ms. Early sighed and shook her head. "Dontel," she said, "I am so sorry."

"But what about the missing space-related snack?" cried Willette. "We were counting on you two to solve *that* mystery! We're starving and now our stop at the rest area will be delayed because of the busted tailpipe!"

"Don't you worry," called Mrs. Marquise back in the direction of Willette. "Mrs. Tango and I will solve the case."

"Do you have any leads?" demanded Siggie.

"Not just yet, but—"

"Children," said Ms. Early, "don't be rude. Thank Mrs. Marquise for trying to find the snack."

"What's going on in here?" Grammy was back on the bus, breathing hard, followed closely by Cyrus.

Everyone brought Grammy and Cyrus up to speed. Cyrus turned his head toward Smashie and shook it slowly.

"*Smashie McPerter,*" Grammy began, but Mrs. Marquise laid a restraining hand on her arm.

"She already feels terrible, Sue. And she's going to investigate."

"I want you all to find the snack first!" Cyrus was quite worked up. "The drawing is probably just back in the classroom in the backpack and cubby area. I think you are making a big deal out of nothing. What we really need is that snack!"

"Yeah!"

"Find the snack first!"

"Please?"

"You people and that snack!" cried Dontel. "Doesn't anybody care about my missing drawing?"

"I do," said Smashie.

Dontel refused to look at her.

"I need a new Investigator Suit before I even work the case," Smashie said sadly. "This red outfit is the worstest-luck one I ever had."

"I'll say," muttered Dontel.

"If you're not going to wear that turban any-more, can I?" asked Joyce shyly from the back seat of the bus across from Mr. Bloom, where she sat with Charlene. "I think it's beautiful."

"Sure," said Smashie dully, and she got up to deliver the turban to Joyce in the rear of the bus. What did she care about her turban when everything was so awful?

"I'm going to go outside to confer with Mr. Potter," said Ms. Early. "You all listen to Mrs. Marquise, Mrs. Tango, and Mr. Bloom while I'm out there—and behave."

"Smashie, can I take the seat next to you?" Charlene asked her. "I'd like to watch your grand-mother do her needlepoint."

"No problem," Smashie said, and crossed paths with Charlene as she threaded her way down the aisle to Joyce. Jacinda got up and followed Smashie.

"I want to look at that turban more closely myself,"

Jacinda admitted, and sat down in Charlene's vacated spot next to Joyce.

Clonk.

"Did you hear that clonk?" asked Smashie as she handed Joyce the turban.

"Woo-hoo for the planetarium trip!" John cried, clearly unable to contain his excitement despite the setback of the broken bus.

Willette joined in. "Yes!" she cried. "Woo-hoo!"

Joyce sighed. "The clonk is probably just something Mr. Potter is doing to the bus. Ooh, this turban is even more beautiful up close!"

"My grammy says it's like something Gloria Swanson would have worn," said Smashie, leaning over the seat to talk to the two girls. "Gloria Swanson was an old-time movie actress."

"She sure was something in her day," said Mr. Bloom from his seat across from Joyce and Jacinda.

"I can't wait to try it on!" said Joyce, wiggling in her seat.

"It helps to pull your ears out from under it," said Smashie. "Keeps it on better."

Joyce settled the red satin headpiece on her own

head, where it promptly fell past her eyes and ears. "I see what you mean," said her lips from underneath.

"I'll help you," said Jacinda with her usual forthright confidence as Smashie returned to her seat. Dontel had left his spot next to his grandmother and had gone to sit farther up in the bus to talk to Alonso.

Will Alonso be mad at me now, too? wondered Smashie sadly. She had always counted Alonso as a good friend.

"Say, Smashie." It was Billy, come to stand beside her. "If you're letting people wear those hats, could I have a turn with that homburg?"

"Really?" said Smashie. "After you've been so terrible to Dontel?"

"What do you care?" asked Billy. "You guys are fighting."

"Well, I don't want to be. And I stick up for my friends."

"You sure he's your friend anymore?" asked Billy. Then he turned away from Smashie and went back to his seat at the back of the bus in front of Mr. Bloom.

Smashie's stomach churned. What if Billy was right? What if she and Dontel never made up? An image of them both, old and gray on rocking chairs, facing each other from their houses across the street but not looking at each other or even waving, swept through Smashie's mind, and her heart sank. It would be terrible to go through life without Dontel.

"Can I wear the homburg?" asked Jacinda, coming up to Smashie's seat. "I'd like a turn with a hat, too."

"Sure," said Smashie. *What do I care about these hats*

when everything's gone so wrong? And, prizing the black hat out of her backpack, she handed it to Jacinda.

"What does the AAM embroidered on it stand for?" asked Jacinda.

"NEVER MIND," said Smashie.

This was surely the most terrible day she had had in her life.

CHAPTER 15

Sent to Mr. Bloom

Miserably, Smashie fished out the last hat from her Brainyon backpack. It was the big fuzzy Russian one—her last chance at an Investigation Suit.

If only it weren't so hot. Smashie's head boiled under the dark pretend fur.

"Smashie," said her grammy, rearing up sternly over the seat back, "I want you to go to the back of the bus and sit with Mr. Bloom."

"Why, Grammy?" said Smashie, startled.

"Because he'll keep an eye on you. I can't keep an eye on you now while I'm investigating the missing space-related snack, and I'm also annoyed with you about stealing Dontel's picture that he worked so hard on and losing it. You have got to learn to be less careless."

Smashie's eyes filled with tears again as she made her way to the back of the bus to sit with Mr. Bloom.

"Don't be teary, Miss McP.," said Mr. Bloom kindly. He handed her a tissue. Smashie wiped her eyes gratefully.

In the seat opposite, Jacinda and Joyce turned to her sympathetically. The turban covered Joyce's whole head, even the thick bangs that she usually hid under. Joyce was much more reserved than Jacinda, but, nonetheless, she seemed excited to be wearing Smashie's hat today.

See? thought Smashie, despite her misery. *Suits give you confidence!*

Joyce moved her head carefully to address Smashie.

"We understand why you're sad, Smash," she said.

"You really wanted to do something nice for Dontel."

Smashie nodded, gulping. "But now he and my grammy are mad at me," she said.

"Don't you worry about that, Miss McP.," Mr. Bloom said. "They'll forgive you."

"Eventually," said Billy, turning around in his seat to address them. He had clearly been listening in. "That's what I've found with you guys, anyway. Even you and Dontel will forgive me at some point."

"Hmmph," said Smashie. But it was a half-hearted *hmmph* due to the weight of her own guilt and sadness.

"You know, Miss McP.," said Mr. Bloom, "Billy's right about one thing. Your grandmother and Dontel are sure to forgive you, so long as you show you've learned your lesson from all this."

"I never learned a lesson harder in my life," said Smashie. "Not even the time I cut myself with the kitchen shears making a How to Open a Done-Up-Too-Tight Package from the United States Post Office Suit."

"This is an out-of-the-blue question, Mr. Bloom,"

said Jacinda from across the aisle. "But why do you call me Miss M. and Joyce Miss C. but Smashie Miss McP.?"

"That's just how you do initials with people who have a McSomething name," explained Mr. Bloom. "Just how it is."

"CRUMBS!"

The shout sounded from the middle of the bus.

Smashie recognized the shouter. It was Grammy. Smashie stood up to see what was going on.

Grammy was leaning over in her seat and picking at something on the floor. "Sniff these," she told Mrs. Marquise, sitting back up and extending her hand to her friend.

Mrs. Marquise sniffed. "Those are definitely crumbs from our cookies," she said. "I'd recognize the scent of that recipe anywhere."

"A clue!" Grammy cried. "DROPPED CRUMBS!"

"Why are you shouting out all our clues?" asked Mrs. Marquise incredulously.

"Because I want the miscreant to know we are onto them!" said Grammy. "I've never been so disappointed in my life. To think a Room 11 child stole those cookies, leaving crumbs all over this floor!"

Willette groaned.

"Do you mean all that's left of our space-related snack?" she asked. "Some dirty old crumbs on the floor?"

"My guess is no, Willette," Mrs. Marquise reassured her. "I think your class thief took one cookie and ate it and shed the crumbs on the floor. Now we just have to work to figure out who."

And she and Grammy bent their heads close to each other again to confer.

Smashie sat down again and adjusted her fuzzy hat.

"That is some hat, Miss McP.," said Mr. Bloom.

"Thank you," said Smashie. "I am hoping it will help make me a good investigator."

"Looks awful toasty," observed Mr. Bloom. Smashie's brow was sweating.

"It is," she said. "But you know how I need suits to solve hard problems, and this is the best I can do with what I brought on the bus."

"I understand completely," said Mr. Bloom. "Used to have a hat like that myself," he added. "Nice and warm in the winter. But the missus just hated it. Took it away from me. Said it gave her the creeps. Like I was wearing a rabbit on my head."

"It does kind of feel like that," said Smashie. "I can't say as how this is my favorite of my three hats."

"Didn't you bring a mustache, too?" asked Billy,

whirling around in his seat again. "I heard you tell Dontel on the playground."

"Yes. But that was a special treat for Dontel only," said Smashie firmly.

"Darn," said Billy. "No hat, no mustache. You really are sore at me this time."

Cyrus appeared in the seat next to Billy. "You can't blame her," he said. "You were pretty terrible about all that stuff with the action figures and the way you messed up Dontel's Brainyon picture."

"All right, all right," said Billy. "I give up."

"I can't even think of how to start investigating," said Smashie to Mr. Bloom, looking miserably at the horse on her Investigation Notebook. "I'm not used to doing it without Dontel."

"It's good to have someone to bounce ideas off of," said Mr. Bloom. "Maybe we can help."

"I'll help," said Joyce immediately.

"Me too," said Cyrus and Jacinda.

"There's nothing else to do while we're waiting for Mr. Potter to finish fixing the bus," Jacinda added.

Smashie was grateful.

I better start with explaining our methodology, she thought, and opened her notebook to the page headed with:

THE MISSING TECHNICALLY CORRECT
DRAWING OF A SPACE ROCKET

CHAPTER 16

Teaching Investigating

"First," said Smashie, "it helps to think about motives. *Why* someone would have committed the crime."

"How come?" asked Joyce.

"Because that often leads you to the culprit."

"And you look for clues, too, right, Smash?" asked Jacinda. Her tone was admiring.

"Yes," said Smashie. "Here, let me show you the Clues List."

"That green smudge is a good one," said Jacinda.

"It sure is," said Smashie, holding up her left index finger. "That's what gave me away to Dontel."

The two girls nodded sympathetically. "Too bad," said Joyce.

"I'm impressed, Miss McP.," said Mr. Bloom.

"I'm going to leave you all to do this investigating stuff," said Billy. "You don't want me around anyway, Smashie." And Billy took his backpack and moved his way up the bus aisle to the seat where John was sitting.

Smashie only rolled her eyes. But she was also relieved, as she wasn't exactly keen for Billy to see he was on the Suspect List.

Jacinda, Joyce, Cyrus, Mr. Bloom, and Smashie leaned over the Investigation Notebook once more.

Smashie couldn't help thinking of Dontel. Her former best friend. Since babyhood. Why, he had been at Smashie's very first birthday party, when she had first been called Smashie instead of—but never mind. That didn't bear thinking of right now. Things were bad enough without yet another reminder today of her awful, terrible real name.

CHAPTER 17
Smudge

"John thinks you ought to forgive me, Smash," said Billy, pushing his way back to the seat in front of Smashie and Mr. Bloom.

As if on cue, John cried, "Yeah, Brainyon says: USE YOUR BRAINS!" And he and Dontel bumped fists diagonally across the aisle at the front of the bus.

"Grr," said Billy. "AHOY THE HADDOCK!" he shouted toward the front of the bus.

"Cut it out," Mr. Bloom called. "You know there's to be no yelling on the bus."

"Sorry," said John.

"Sorry," said Billy.

"Smashie," said Jacinda, "Joyce and I were both wondering what this embroidered AAM means—"

Smashie cut her right off.

"Never mind." She looked Jacinda in the eye. "Sorry," she said. "But I thought we were still investigating here."

"Smashie and Jacinda," said Cyrus, "could I have a turn with that homburg? I kind of think I need an Investigation Suit, too."

"Sure," said Smashie and Jacinda in unison, and Cyrus took the hat from Jacinda and plonked it on his own head. With one hand, he moved the hat to sit more on the back of his head and held it there so he could still see.

"I better collect some child-size hats in the future," said Smashie. "Wearing adult ones is like trying to keep bandages off your eyes. You can't see what's right in front of you." And she pushed her own hot furry hat further back on her own head as well.

"I bet that Russian hat would fit me," said Mr. Bloom. "Got a head as big as a watermelon, I do."

"Why, Mr. Bloom," said Smashie, "would you like a turn with this hat?"

"I kind of would," admitted the custodian. Smashie handed it over.

"Wow," said Billy.

"Neat," said Cyrus.

They were right. Mr. Bloom looked terrific in the hat.

"Why, if I didn't have to mind you, I'd go show your grammy," said Mr. Bloom. "But I have to stay glued by your side, Miss McP."

"Miss McP.," repeated Jacinda musingly. "Miss McP." She turned and said something to Joyce that Smashie couldn't quite catch. Oh, well. It was rude to listen in, anyway.

Clonk.

Another clonk, thought Smashie, and sure enough, Mr. Potter heaved himself back onto the bus. "Good as new," he said, taking his seat.

The bus erupted in cheers.

"Hooray for the planetarium trip!" cried Charlene.

"Huzzah for fixing the bus!" cried Alonso.

John grinned his satisfaction.

"We'll still have time to stop at the rest stop for our space-related snack!" said Willette. "That is, if anyone ever finds it."

"We're still on the job," Mrs. Marquise reassured her, and Willette sighed.

"It's like they don't trust you and Dontel to investigate the cookie mystery," said Jacinda.

"Well, we can't solve a mystery together when we're fighting and seated at opposite ends of the bus," Smashie pointed out.

"I'm going to quick go show Charlene this homburg before we get going," said Cyrus. And off he went.

Clonk.

"Mr. Bloom," said Smashie, "I don't like the sound of those clonks. Do you think the bus is really repaired?"

"These old buses make a lot of sounds," Mr. Bloom reassured her. "Don't you worry. Mr. Potter is a first-rate bus tender, and he wouldn't take a chance with the bus if he thought it wasn't safe."

Smashie was comforted. But there was still the mystery of the missing drawing to tend to.

There was a great cough from the bus as its engine started again, and finally Room 11 was chugging along the road again at last.

"I am so excited about this trip!" Cyrus cried from his spot beside Charlene.

"Me too," said Charlene. "Even though this is already the longest bus ride in the world."

"Going to be even longer," said Mr. Bloom. "The planetarium is still a ways away."

"Grargh," said Jacinda. "I'm dying to be there already! But all these mysteries sure are keeping us hopping."

"Are you guys going to keep working on the mystery?" Billy asked Smashie, swiveling his head around. "Ugh. I get kind of bus sick turning around when the bus is in motion."

"You do get green around the gills easily," said Joyce sympathetically.

"I know," said Billy. "It's my whole family's fatal flaw."

Smashie started. She didn't know other families had fatal flaws as her own did, what with her grammy, mother, and Smashie herself being hasty and having to fix up their fix-its all the time. Why, wasn't that what Smashie was doing right now?

"We were looking at clues," said Joyce.

"Ohhhhh," moaned Billy, taking his hands off the seat back and turning back around to face front. "I *am* getting green around the gills. I hate bus sickness!"

"So do I," said Mr. Bloom. "Used to get sick something awful when I was a boy."

And Billy was certainly green. But that was not the only thing that was. For before he had taken his hands off the seat, Smashie had seen a smudge on his right thumb.

A green smudge.

Smashie wriggled in her seat with joy. She was about to bring a prime suspect to light!

CHAPTER 18

Searching Belongings

This is terrific! thought Smashie. *I can tax Billy and then frog-march him up to the front of the bus when we stop at the rest stop for the snack that we won't have on account of its being missing! Billy will give back the drawing, admit to whatever motive he had for taking it, and then Dontel will be my best friend again!*

"Billy Kamarski," said Smashie in her sharpest voice, "don't you use nausea as an excuse. I saw that green smudge on your hand!"

"Green smudge?"

"On Billy's hand?"

Joyce and Jacinda were incredulous.

"I do not have a green smudge," said Billy as stoutly as he could through his nausea.

"Prove it," said Smashie tersely. "Show us your hands."

"I can't turn around without barfing," moaned Billy.

"Miss McP.," said Mr. Bloom, "are you sure about this?"

"As sure as I've ever been," said Smashie.

"Well, then, Mr. K.," said Mr. Bloom, "suppose you face front and hold your hands up in the air for us to see."

"Fine," said Billy, and he held up his hands so the backs were to the investigators.

No smudge.

"Turn them the other way," Smashie ordered.

Slowly, reluctantly, Billy turned them the other way.

And there it was. A green marker smudge on his right thumb.

"*Aha!*" cried Smashie. "You have Dontel's drawing!"

"Now, Miss McP., don't get ahead of yourself," warned Mr. Bloom. "We've already had a lot of drama on this bus."

"Well, I have proof!" shouted Smashie. Heads from the bus turned back toward her.

"Have you found our snack?" yelled Alonso back hopefully.

"No yelling on my bus," called Mr. Potter firmly.

"Sorry, Mr. Potter!" said Smashie. "And nope, Alonso! Still working on that."

Smashie turned to her fellow investigators and lowered her voice. But it was no less severe for being more quiet.

"Not only do you have the smudge, Billy," she said, "but you also had a motive. And you had opportunity!"

"I did not!" cried Billy, still facing front to control his upset stomach.

"You did," said Smashie relentlessly. "Your opportunity"—she thumped her notebook with her hand—"was when the whole class was racing around looking for the missing space-related snack and you were by the backpack pile! Why, you were the one who found the tote bag there!"

"Who cares!" cried Billy. "And what kind of motive do you think I'd have, anyway? What would I do with an old technically correct drawing of a space rocket? Why would I want it?"

"To The Haddock it up," said Smashie firmly. "And," she added, "for revenge." She reached over the seat until her Investigation Notebook was in front of Billy's greenish face and tapped the motive she and Dontel had written down earlier:

1. Revenge for getting in trouble about Brainyon

"I don't have it, I tell you!" Billy was really upset. "Ohh, I really might barf."

"Ease up on the boy, Miss McP.," said Mr. Bloom.

"Certainly," said Smashie. *"If he lets us search his belongings."*

"Fine," moaned Billy. "Then search my darned

belongings! See if I care!" And, still facing stoutly to the front, he held up his backpack for Smashie to take.

"I don't know as how I like this, Miss McP.," said Mr. Bloom.

"Billy doesn't mind," said Joyce.

"Yes," agreed Jacinda. "Why shouldn't we? Let's get to it. Unzip the bag, Smashie."

Smashie unzipped the bag. She took out Billy's math homework. She took out an orange that had clearly been living in the backpack for some time. And then her hand closed on something hard. She pulled it out slowly.

"Did you find the tube?" Jacinda asked breathlessly.

"No," said Smashie. "I found Billy's The Haddock."

CHAPTER 19

Green Around the Gills

"Now, Mr. K.," said Mr. Bloom disapprovingly, "I happen to know you are under a two-week ban from bringing that The Haddock figure into school. Why do you have it in your backpack?"

"I couldn't resist," cried Billy. "And my two weeks is up tomorrow. I didn't want to forget my The Haddock on the day I was allowed to have him, so I just stuck him in there. I wasn't going to take him out, honest."

Smashie brushed the matter of The Haddock to one side, handing the action figure to Mr. Bloom. "That's all well and good," she said in her best taxing voice. Taxing suspects was not only one of Smashie's favorite instances of Investigator Language: it had also always been one of her and Dontel's favorite things to do when they worked a case. A wave of sadness washed over her now as she wished Dontel were with her to share this moment and join her in taxing Billy. But she pressed on. "What about that smudge?" she demanded.

"There are other green markers in the world, you know," said Billy. "I used one of Ms. Early's to make a sign to put on Siggie's back in the bus line yesterday afternoon. SMACK ME UPSIDE THE HEAD, it said."

"So if I were to ask Ms. Early, she'd say she lent you her marker yesterday?" *I am being terribly relentless,* thought Smashie proudly.

Billy wilted. He gulped. "Well," he said, "I didn't exactly ask her for her green marker."

"You mean you just took it?" Smashie was aghast. Surely there was a lot of crime afoot and she herself was a thief, but to steal from a teacher!

"I guess I did," said Billy. "Now can you all please leave me alone for a minute because I really am going to barf. Why do there have to be so many potholes on this road?" he wailed.

It was true. The bus ride was very bumpy going.

But Smashie couldn't pay attention to the bumping. She was crushed. She'd thought she'd solved the mystery and here she was, back to square one.

"That was good investigating, anyway, Smashie," said Joyce sympathetically. "Billy really did fit all those clues. Sorry, Billy," she added with a concerned glance diagonally across the aisle at her green classmate.

"Do you need a plastic bag, Billy?" asked Jacinda. "Because I have one in my backpack."

"Just please stop talking to me for a while," Billy said desperately, and looked resolutely forward.

"Poor kid," said Mr. Bloom. "Good thing we'll be at that rest stop soon."

Billy may be a poor kid for being so sick, Smashie thought. But he wasn't the one who had lost his best friend.

What could she do to win back Dontel's friendship?

she wondered. Hire a marching band to parade in front of his house and sing "I Am Sorry, Dontel!" songs? Smashie pictured herself in a Majorette Suit with a baton, marching and singing earnestly at the front of a cavalcade. Or maybe she could hire a sky-writer to write I AM SORRY, DONTEL! in the sky over his house!

But Smashie knew neither of those would work. Apologies were not enough. The only possible way to heal the rift in the friendship would be for her to find Dontel's technically correct drawing of a space rocket that she was responsible for losing.

CHAPTER 20

Not Giving Up

DR. REBECCA LEE CRUMPLER

"Miss McP.," said Mr. Bloom beside her, "you're not thinking of giving up the case, are you?"

"Maybe you should investigate the missing cookies instead!" said Joyce eagerly. "Don't you want a delicious space-related snack at the rest stop?"

"Please stop talking about food," groaned Billy.

Smashie was silent.

"It's Dontel's rocket plans you want to investigate, isn't it?" said Mr. Bloom in a low voice. "Don't think

I don't know how badly you're feeling, Miss McP. Why, I'll still help you."

"You will?" said Smashie. "You'll help me work the case? Even though I messed up with Billy?"

"Well, we got his The Haddock," said Mr. Bloom, waggling the action figure fishily at Smashie. "So it wasn't all in vain. Let's get going with this case. Never give up—that's my motto. Why, the people I admire most never gave up. Especially not when the going got hard."

"That's what Dontel always says he learned from Dr. Cornelius DuVasse Bryson's books," said Smashie sadly.

"You know who I look up to who never gave up?" Mr. Bloom asked.

"Who?" said Smashie.

"Dr. Rebecca Lee Crumpler."

"You mean the lady our school was named for?"

"Yep, indeedy," said Mr. Bloom. "She was the first African American female physician in the United States. She cared an awful lot about people and helped a lot of them, too. And a lot of ignorant types tormented her. Said the MD after her name stood for

Mule Driver instead of *Medical Doctor*. And did that stop her? No. She doctored her heart out anyway. Now, *that's* not giving up. And you're not going to give up, either."

"Wow," said Smashie. "No wonder you look up to Dr. Crumpler."

"Good," said Mr. Bloom. "Then make her proud and keep investigating the disappearance of that drawing. Use the brains you were given and do your best. That's all anyone can ask for."

"You sound like Ms. Early." For the first time in what seemed like hours, Smashie smiled. "Ms. Early is who I look up to," she added shyly. "And also my mom and grandmother. And Dontel's."

"Why, that's wonderful," said Mr. Bloom. "Everybody ought to have at least one person to look up to."

"Charlene looks up to her mother," said Smashie, sitting up straighter in her seat. "And I know John looks up to his dad."

"See?" said Mr. Bloom. "So just think of Ms. Early and all she taught you and those grandmothers up there investigating those cookies and Dr. Crumpler doctoring like billy-o and do your darnedest to find Dontel's technically correct drawing of a space rocket."

Smashie slumped in her seat. "I *am* thinking of my grammy," she said. "And she is mad at me, too. What if more people get mad at me? What if my mom is even mad at me after we get home and Grammy tells her about today?"

"Don't you worry, Miss McP. They still love you."

But how could Mr. Bloom know? Smashie could not bear the thought of getting off the bus at the rest stop and confronting the angry, disappointed face of her grandmother once more.

CHAPTER 21

Rest Stop

But that didn't bear thinking about right now.

"All right, children!" called Ms. Early to the sea of red-hoodied, blue-jeaned children from the front of the bus as it stopped with a clonk.

"Hooray for field-trip rest stops!" cried Willette.

"Huzzah!"

"That's right." Ms. Early nodded. "We are at the rest stop. You can use the restrooms and run around a bit under the watchful eyes of our chaperones.

We've been on this bus quite a while, and, although you were all very patient while the tailpipe was fixed, I must say it's been a rather dramatic ride." She paused and glanced at Cyrus in the homburg, Jacinda in the turban, and Mr. Bloom in the fuzzy Russian hat.

"Let us leave these hats here," said Mr. Bloom.

"Thank you," said Smashie. "I wouldn't want them to get all smooshed."

And the three laid the hats down on their seats before joining the line of children standing ready to get off the bus. Ms. Early got off first to stand beside Mr. Potter with her clipboard.

"I wish we were already at the planetarium," declared Willette. "I can't wait!"

Cyrus beamed.

"Ugh!" said Alonso as Smashie and the other back-of-the-bus children neared his seat. "I can't get my backpack out from under the seat."

"Pull harder," said Dontel.

Smashie tried to catch Dontel's eye but she could not.

She drew herself up.

Mom. Grammy. Dr. Crumpler.

Never give up.

And Smashie went resolutely forward. *Dontel and I will be friends again. We will!*

"I *am* pulling harder," said Alonso. "Go on without me, Dontel. I'll get it. I feel dumb with the whole bus watching me try."

Leaping from the last step of the bus into the sunshine of the day was heaven. It was a lovely day and a lovely rest stop, full of trees and grass and picnic tables. Other schools on their way to the planetarium clearly had had the same idea, and some groups of children in blue and green hoodies sat at picnic tables with their adults at the far end of the rest stop.

"We would have had our snack here," said Willette to Smashie sadly as they sat down with Billy and Tatiana at one of their own picnic tables. Dontel was seated at another with John and Joyce, facing the bus with his back to Smashie.

"We sure would have," said Cyrus from across the way. "Too bad our space-related snack hasn't been found."

Should Smashie approach Dontel and try to

apologize once more? She could fill him in about her sort of terrible work with the investigation, and then maybe he would see how much better they functioned as a team.

Gingerly, Smashie approached his table.

"Dontel?" she said.

Her voice wobbled.

Dontel turned and looked her straight in the eyes.

Then slowly, deliberately, he turned his back on her.

His feelings toward Smashie were palpable. Blinking back tears, she made her way back to the table where Willette, Billy, and Tatiana sat. Everything was still terrible.

Dontel had not forgiven her.

Tatiana unzipped her hoodie against the warm sunshine of the day, and Smashie caught sight of the T-shirt she wore underneath. NASA, it said.

That stands for National Aeronautics and Space Administration, thought Smashie. *They're the ones who go into space.* She sat bolt upright, her tears drying in an instant. For that meant that Tatiana *liked space*!

Maybe she liked it so much that she stole Dontel's drawing!

An image of Tatiana tiptoeing back to the backpack area to steal the drawing filled Smashie's mind. What was Tatiana planning to do with it? Make it life-size and put herself in Brainyon's cockpit and zoom to outer space? Or send the craft out as it was to try to pick up alien communication signals? Who knew, but Smashie was sure she was onto something. And if she was right, she'd get that drawing back and she and Dontel would make up and he really would be her best friend again.

It was time to tax Tatiana.

"Tatiana," she began in her sternest voice, "why are you wearing that NASA shirt?"

Tatiana stared at her. "Because I like it," she said. "And we're going to the planetarium today. Why do you ask?"

"No reason," said Smashie, but she pegged Tatiana with a look. "Where were you this morning when we were looking for the lost space-related snack?"

Tatiana stared at her some more. "Are you taxing me?" she asked. "Because I am not going to let you tax me."

"I'm just asking," said Smashie.

But Tatiana sealed her lips firmly, and, although Smashie peppered her with questions about her whereabouts and the degree to which Tatiana liked space, Tatiana refused to say a word.

Suspicious! thought Smashie. *I am putting Tatiana on my Suspects List as soon as we get back on that bus! Only a big stealie-pants would refuse to answer questions!* And she sat up, bold and resolute.

Alonso, backpack on his back at last, jumped out of the bus and joined Smashie and the others at their table.

"Don't you guys want to run around?" Cyrus asked them. "I sure do. Let's play tag."

"I'm staying put awhile," said Alonso.

"Come on, Smashie. Play with us this once," begged Cyrus.

And even though Smashie was not the fastest runner in the world and had yet to mark her suspicions of Tatiana down in her Investigation Notebook, she decided to join the game. "Got to get my yayas out," she explained to Alonso. She had more yayas than ever after her taxing of Tatiana.

And she ran off as Alonso and Billy, who also did not want to play tag, grew deep in conversation with Tatiana.

Even more suspicious! thought Smashie. *Tatiana is talking with Billy, a former A-number-one suspect!*

"Gotcha, Smash!" cried Siggie, who was It, as he flashed past her.

"Darn," said Smashie. She went over to join the adults at their picnic table, which had been designated as the Out table by the tag players. But she was not eager to do so. For once Mr. Potter wasn't annoyed with her, but Grammy had not yet forgiven her about Dontel's drawing. She drew up beside her grammy without a word.

"See? It's good to get your yayas out," said Grammy. She reached around and hugged Smashie to her by the waist. "I'm sorry I made you feel so bad," she said. "You were wrong to take the picture and to plan on breaking rule four, but I know you only meant the best for your friend. Forgive me, Smashie?"

"Forgive *you*?" said Smashie incredulously. "Of course! I was afraid you wouldn't forgive *me*!"

And she sat down beside her grammy and they hugged some more.

"I love you," said Grammy.

"I love you, too," said Smashie.

Grammy took her needlepoint out of her bag. *Punk, punk, punk* went her needle as it pierced the fabric over and over again. "Why don't you come back and sit up by me again when get back on the bus?" Grammy suggested.

"Can I stay with Mr. Bloom instead?" asked Smashie. "He's . . . helping me."

"Why, surely," said Grammy. "That's fine." And she beamed across the table at Mr. Bloom.

Good, thought Smashie. Grammy had an eagle eye, and if Smashie ever got her hands back on the tube containing Dontel's technically correct drawing of a space rocket, there'd be no escaping her to find Dr. Bryson's best friend in the meeting at the planetarium. For that was Smashie's new, revised plan. The planetarium was huge, and Smashie suspected it would not be so easy to find the meeting area where Dr. Bryson's best friend was talking with the other heads of planetariums. Smashie imagined heads of planetariums didn't sit in a circle on the floor right by the door the way Room 11 did. No, they would be meeting in some big, important chamber, and Smashie would have to find it in that huge building all by herself as she indeed broke rule four, and the trust of her grandmother and her teacher.

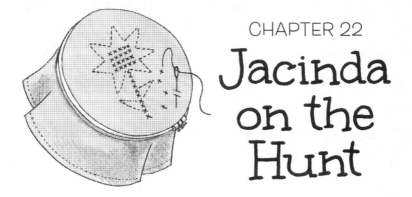

CHAPTER 22

Jacinda on the Hunt

"That's a gorgeous design, Mrs. Tango," Ms. Early said, leaning over to look at Granny's needlepoint hoop.

"With no curves!" shouted Jacinda as she ran past Smashie's Grammy in the tag game.

"You said it, girl!" called Grammy after she and Jacinda laughed, even as Siggie took advantage of her distraction and tagged her.

Jacinda joined Smashie at the table with the adults.

"Mrs. Tango," said Jacinda purposefully, "what is Smashie's real name?"

A silence fell over the table.

Smashie broke it.

"You know I never tell!" she cried to Jacinda. "Why, you've known that since kindergarten! I thought I finally had everybody trained not to ask!"

"I can't think why, though," said Mrs. Marquise. "It's such a pretty—"

"IT IS NOT," said Smashie.

"I think we should respect Smashie's wishes," said Ms. Early. "After all, her name is her business, and we all have known her only as Smashie for years."

"I agree," said Grammy.

Smashie sagged with relief. "Thank you," she said.

"I got a clue, though," said Jacinda. "And I'm going to start guessing."

"Jacinda," said Ms. Early warningly.

"Sorry," said Jacinda. "Couldn't help myself."

But something in the way Jacinda said "Sorry" told Smashie that, this time, Jacinda was not backing off, even though she and Smashie were good friends and Smashie had let Jacinda wear the red turban for so much of the trip. Jacinda had figured out something about Smashie's name and was going to try to use what she knew to find out the truth.

Smashie wished she hadn't taught Jacinda quite so much about investigating.

CHAPTER 23
Ersatz Suit

"Ms. Early," said Willette, coming over to the grown-ups' table, "may I go get my thermos off the bus? I'm thirsty from all that running around."

"Certainly," said Ms. Early, and off Willette went.

All around Smashie, Room 11 ran and tagged and laughed.

But after a few minutes, Mr. Potter shouted, "Room 11, time to get on the bus!" and the children stopped running and talking and started to heave themselves back onto the bus instead.

Smashie took her seat next to Mr. Bloom. Not

only did she want to sit next to him anyway, but it would also be good to keep an eye on Jacinda, at least until this name thing quieted down a bit. Then Smashie could relax into investigating the missing rocket plans for real.

When she reached her seat, Jacinda and Joyce were already in their spots across the aisle. Jacinda was talking animatedly. But she stopped when she saw Smashie.

"Smashie," she said purposefully, "may I have a turn again with the homburg?"

"Hey," said Cyrus. "I was wearing that."

"I think everyone should keep the hats they have," said Smashie firmly.

"But can't I *please* have a turn with that turban?" said Billy. "Ahoy The Haddock!"

"What does my turban have to do with The Haddock, for heaven's sake?" said Smashie.

"Nothing," Billy admitted. "I just like shouting that."

"You haven't even apologized for what you did to Dontel's stuff the other week," said Smashie.

"Oh, fine," said Billy. "I apologize for taking his action figure."

"What about defacing his drawing?" Smashie demanded.

There was an agonized silence from Billy.

"See?" said Smashie. "No turban for you!"

"No wonder you like suits so much, Smashie," said Joyce. "It feels wonderful to dress up, even if it's just a hat. Especially today, when we're all dressed alike. Makes you feel, well, *different.*"

"That's exactly it," Smashie agreed. "It makes you feel like another part of you is in the front of your brain. And that's the part that helps you solve hard problems!"

"Hey, where is that turban, anyway?" asked Jacinda. "I don't see it anywhere!"

"It was right here on our seat," said Joyce. Her voice was worried. "Smashie, I think we lost your turban!"

"OR DID YOU?" cried Billy. "I can investigate as well as anybody! I bet you took it, and the motive is on account of you loving it so much! See? You aren't the only ones detecting people around here!" And he sat back, heaving.

Joyce blinked. "Why would we steal it when Smashie was letting us wear it as much as we wanted?" she asked.

"Yeah," said Jacinda, angry. "Smashie, we really didn't—"

"I know," said Smashie. "Don't worry. It'll turn up. I lose things all the time."

"Mr. K., apologize to the girls."

"Oh, fine," said Billy. "I'm sorry."

But Smashie was too distracted to take in the apology. *I really need to get back to investigating the missing technically correct drawing of the space rocket! But how?* It occurred to Smashie that she had no suit right now to take on the investigation. What could she use?

Jacinda and Joyce seemed to read her mind.

"I have a scarf in my bag," said Jacinda.

"I have a pair of gloves," said Joyce, now in the homburg with the AAM stitched onto the side. "They're my mom's, so they're pretty big, but they might look like investigator gloves if you wore them. They are black pretend leather."

Smashie looked at the girls gratefully and relaxed for the first time since she'd gotten on the bus. This proffered suit would do for anybody, investigation-wise.

"Thank you," she told the girls. Then she wound the scarf around her neck and crossed it over her torso like a sash. She put on the gloves. They were large and flappy but Smashie pushed that problem to one side and thought instead of her mother, her grandmother, Ms. Early, and Dr. Crumpler.

She was ready for anything.

CHAPTER 24

Found and Lost

But despite her new Investigator Suit, or maybe because of it, a wave of missing Dontel washed over Smashie. Was he missing her, too, up there near the front of the bus with Alonso?

"FROSTING!" boomed a familiar voice from up near the middle of the bus. Grammy.

"Frosting?" came Ms. Early's puzzled voice. She paused in her counting of the children in their seats.

"FROSTING ON THE BACK OF THIS SEAT!"

bellowed Grammy once more into the quiet of the not-yet-moving bus.

"And so there is," said John, leaning back to see. "How did that get there?"

"Not only *how*, young man," said Grammy. "But by *whom*."

"'By whom'?" repeated John.

"By whom," said Grammy firmly. "This frosting is the exact burst of color we used to create the supernovas on some of those missing cookies! That means the miscreant ate a cookie *and in so doing smeared frosting on the back of this seat by mistake!*"

Mrs. Marquise pinched the bridge of her nose and shook her head.

"What's a supernova?" asked Cyrus.

"It's when a certain kind of star explodes at the end of its life," explained Mr. Bloom. "It grows purely massive and throws out clouds of gas and other material into the galaxy before it shrinks to almost nothing."

"But that's not what matters," said Grammy. "What matters is that the miscreant was here during our break at the rest stop and helped themself to one of the space-related snacks!"

"Which suggests several things," murmured Mrs. Marquise. "Sue—"

"ONE!" boomed Grammy. "The miscreant is among us still! TWO, the miscreant was on this bus during our break! And THREE, the missing snack *is still on this bus!*"

"Sue, why must you always shout our clues?" sighed Mrs. Marquise. "How will we ever catch the perpetrator if you keep putting them on guard?"

Oooh, perpetrator, thought Smashie pleasurably. *I forgot about that piece of Investigator Language!* And she smiled. Looking up, she caught Dontel's eye. He was eyeing her, too. Smashie's heart leaped.

But then he looked away.

Smashie's heart fell.

"I thought Smashie and Dontel were investigating the cookies," said John. "Come on, you two. Help us find that snack!"

"Twelve children present and accounted for, Mr. Potter," Ms. Early said with a sigh. "We can go."

And Mr. Potter threw the bus into reverse and pulled out of the rest stop at last.

Clonk.

"Did you hear the bus clonk again, Mr. Bloom?" asked Smashie.

"Nothing to worry about, Miss McP.," said Mr. Bloom. "I promise. Just an old bus."

"No big deal," said Jacinda, who was now in the homburg.

"That's right," agreed Cyrus. "Why, once my mom—" But before he could finish reassuring Smashie, Grammy's voice boomed once again over the chatter and noise of the bus.

"THE MISSING SPACE-RELATED SNACK!" she shouted. "THE PLASTIC CONTAINER JUST SMACKED MRS. MARQUISE IN THE SNEAKERS!"

"How?"

"What?"

"Who?"

"Ugh!"

The bus erupted once more into a morass of heaving questions.

"Are you saying that the cookies have been found, Mrs. Marquise and Mrs. Tango?" asked Ms. Early.

"Well, Sue was more shouting it than saying it,"

said Mrs. Marquise dryly, "but that's about the size of it."

"Room 11," said Ms. Early sternly, intending to bring everyone back to order. "I am not pleased AT ALL with this proof that someone took the cookies and snuck them to eat on the bus. Why, those cookies were for all the children to enjoy! Were you going to keep them all to yourself?" Ms. Early's voice was full of disappointment and disbelief. "Pass those cookies up here, please," she said.

"Can we eat them, Ms. Early?"

"Please?"

"Just one?"

"Not on my bus," said Mr. Potter wearily. "I know what that'll mean. Frosting and crumbs all over."

"I hate to reward the child who took the cookies with one," said Ms. Early. "But that's really not fair to the rest of you. And I will assign two bus monitors to sweep up the crumbs, Mr. Potter."

Mr. Potter sighed. "All right," he said. "As long as you don't mess up my good clean bus."

"Hooray!" shouted the bus.

And the plastic container began to make its way through the rows of bus seats and into the waiting hands of the hungry third-graders as Mr. Potter threw the bus into forward gear and got back out on the main road with another clonk.

"That snack'll give you sustenance for your own investigation," said Mr. Bloom warmly to Smashie. "One mystery out of the way, even if unsolved, and—"

"Yeah," said Billy. "That cookie mystery is still unsolved. We don't know who took them or anything! Smashie, you didn't really investigate that!"

"No," snapped Smashie. "I was busy investigating YOU."

"All right, all right," said Joyce. "No more fighting. We got the cookies back regardless." She sounded resigned.

"I can't wait to get to the planetarium!" cried Willette.

"Me, either," said Dontel from the front.

"It sure is taking a long time for those cookies to get back here," said Jacinda, straining her neck to see who had the container now. But all over the bus were questioning heads. A few children had cookies, but most did not. And the ones who did not were not pleased.

"Cut it out, you guys up front!"

"Pass them back like Ms. Early said to!"

But the confusion only increased.

"Stop this nonsense," said Ms. Early in her sternest voice. "Who has those cookies?"

But it was no use.

The cookies had disappeared again.

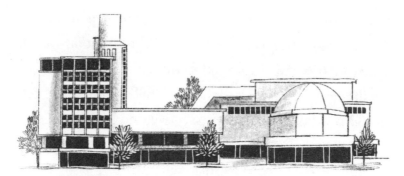

CHAPTER 25

Another Plan

"Room 11," said Ms. Early, "I am very disappointed in you. I have half a mind to turn around and take you straight back to school."

"It wasn't all of us, Ms. Early!"

"It's just one cookie-obsessed thief!"

"Dontel and Smashie! You two have to put your differences to one side and solve this case!" shouted Willette. She seemed almost happy that the cookies were gone.

Why, that's not it, Smashie realized. *Willette thinks*

that the mystery of the missing space-related snack will make me and Dontel stop fighting. She thinks that we will make up if we work together again.

"Please!" said Alonso, biting his lip. "I don't feel good on this bus with a space-related snack thief on it. We need you to find the culprit!"

"Yes, we do!" said John.

"Well, if that doesn't make us feel like chopped liver as detectives, I don't know what will," said Mrs. Marquise.

"Never were truer words spoken," said Grammy.

"It's not that we don't trust you, Mrs. Marquise and Mrs. Tango," said John. "It's just that we are used to Dontel and Smashie doing our detecting."

Smashie looked forward at Dontel.

Dontel looked backward at Smashie.

Neither knew what to say.

"Come on, you guys." John was pleading. "Please? For the good of Room 11?"

There was a pause. Smashie hardly dared to hope. For if they worked on the cookie mystery, why, then she could tell Dontel all about the green smudge on

Billy's thumb and how she had fingered him as the culprit (*Oooh! "Finger as the culprit"! More Investigator Language we'll be able to write down!*) as well as bring him up to speed on Tatiana's refusal to speak and Smashie's own lost turban. And Dontel could share his own findings with her, for she was sure he had not stopped working the case, either, from the front of the bus.

Smashie held her breath.

But, "I think our grandmas are on the job," said Dontel. "I'd rather investigate my missing drawing. On my own."

The bus groaned and clutched at its hair.

"It's okay, Room 11," said Smashie, beating back disappointment. "Our grandmothers are really smart."

"But you two are the best investigators ever!" cried Charlene. "And all of us know it!"

"Let's stop this bickering this minute," said Ms. Early. "Our chaperones have kindly agreed to help us and that is that. Besides, all this will lead to is breaking rule number one—getting out of your seats on the moving bus—and I can't be having with that at all. So. Those of you that have cookies, what do you think would be the kind thing to do?"

"Share," said those children, and they immediately began breaking the cookies into pieces to pass back to the other children.

"You are a good, kind class at heart," said Ms. Early, almost as if to herself.

"More crumbs on my bus," muttered Mr. Potter.

"I'll be a bus monitor," said Siggie.

"So will I!" said Smashie. "Before we even get off the bus at the planetarium!"

"Thank you, children," said Ms. Early. "I knew I could count on you. And look, here we are, practically there!"

It was true. Everyone craned their necks toward the windows to see the glorious, beautiful building sprawling along the road up ahead.

But Smashie only plucked at the sleeve of her red Rebecca Lee Crumpler Elementary School hoodie. *I bet Dontel is thinking about how Dr. Bryson's best friend is in there*, she thought.

"Don't be sad, Miss McP.," said Mr. Bloom. "I have a feeling this argument with young Mr. M. will blow over once you two have a chance to talk to each other face-to-face and hash it out. Why, you kids are two peas in a pod."

"I hope we can be again," said Smashie. "I just wanted to help him."

The bus stopped and Mr. Potter opened the door. The children stood up to get in line to file out.

"Don't you forget to sweep my bus," said Mr. Potter. "All those extra crumbs."

"Siggie," said Smashie suddenly, "don't worry about helping. I can sweep the bus by myself."

"For real, Smash?" asked Siggie. "That is awful nice of you."

"I don't mind," said Smashie. And she didn't. For once more, she had a plan.

CHAPTER 26

Hard Work
Pays Off

"We're here!"

"Hooray!"

"Let's go!"

Ms. Early held up a restraining hand. "I just want to remind people of rules three, four, and five," she said, glancing at Smashie, who looked down. "And two, as we'll be met inside the planetarium by the docent assigned to us and I want you to greet that docent nicely."

"What's a docent?" asked Cyrus.

"Docents are guides in a museum," Ms. Early explained. "They have great knowledge of the exhibits and can answer any questions we may have. Last, there are to be no hats worn in the planetarium." Her eye rested on Smashie again.

"No worries, Ms. Early!" said Smashie. "I'll leave the homburg and my fuzzy Russian hat right here on my seat. May I have the little bus broom, Mr. Potter?" she asked the bus driver as the class headed down the bus stairs.

"Right there on the hook." Mr. Potter nodded to the wall next to his seat, and Smashie crawled across to take up the broom.

Sweep, sweep, sweep! Smashie swept the empty bus as if demon-possessed. For she needed time for her plan.

The cookies must have hit Mrs. Marquise in the sneakers from under a bus seat, she reasoned. Therefore (oooh, "therefore" means I am thinking in Investigator Language)—therefore, it stands to reason that Dontel's tube really might have rolled out of my backpack and be under a bus seat even as we speak!

Smashie hardly dared hope. But hope she did, even though Room 11 had already checked around for Dontel's tube. They would not have been as thorough in their search as Smashie would be now.

She knew the tube had not come back as far as the last row of seats, where she and Mr. Bloom had sat with Jacinda and Joyce across the aisle. But beyond that she couldn't be sure. *What would Dontel do?* she thought. The answer came almost immediately. *Be methodical.* And so would she. Willette had sat in the next row up, so Smashie would start looking there. It made sense anyway, since the forward motion of a bus tended to make things roll backward more often than forward.

Smashie was hopeful. But more than hopeful, she was excited for the special way she planned to look under the seats.

I knew it would come in handy, even if Dontel says I haven't got the knees for it! I can get a much better view of what's under those seats if I dangle!

Thus, the sweeping finished, she stood by the seat in front of Willette's, because its seat back would lend the best vantage point to look under Willette's seat when Smashie dangled down backward from it. Cautiously, she climbed up, hoping Ms. Early would not look through the window and see her. Then she balanced carefully with her knees hooked over the seat top, hanging on with her hands while her rear sank downward in front of where Willette had been positioned.

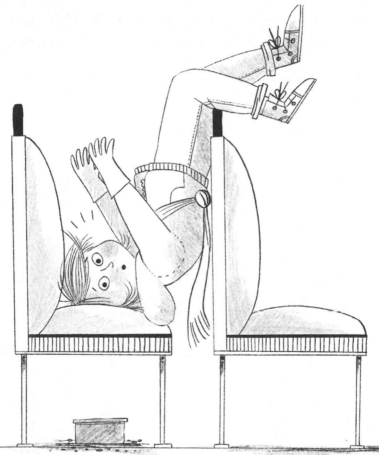

Then Smashie let go.

"UGH!"

She had hit her head on the seat on the way down.

That is the price of trying to conquer injustice, Smashie thought. Also, *ow.*

But it was worth it. For, her head freed, Smashie had a clear view of the space beneath where Willette had sat. And what she saw there shocked her.

A container. A plastic container. Containing space-related snacks.

CHAPTER 27

Smashie in Trouble

"SMASHIE MCPERTER!"

The yell came at the same time as Smashie felt hands reach under her head to support it while an arm lifted her knees off the seat back. It was Grammy. She swooped Smashie up and over the seat and stood her in the aisle of the bus.

"How did you sneak up on me like that?" Smashie cried.

"WHAT IN THE SAM HILL WERE YOU DOING, DANGLING LIKE THAT FROM THE

SEAT BACK?" Grammy was shouting, but Smashie could tell she was worried, not angry.

"I was fine, Grammy," Smashie tried to reassure her. "I've been practicing my dangling and guess what!"

"Guess, nothing," said Grammy. "Out. March." And, as Smashie had pictured her own self doing to many a perp, Grammy marched her down the aisle and out of the bus to receive her comeuppance.

"Ms. Early," said Grammy to that weary teacher, "I am very sorry to have to tell you that I just found my disobedient granddaughter DANGLING FROM A SEAT BACK ON THAT BUS."

"Oh, Smashie," said Ms. Early. "Trust you to break rule number one in such an unusual way. Not to mention dangerous!"

"The bus wasn't even moving!" said Smashie wildly. "Don't you even want to know why I was doing it?"

"No!" said Grammy, Ms. Early, and Mr. Potter in unison.

"There is no reason in the world good enough for doing something so dangerous," said Ms. Early severely. "Why, you could have broken your neck if you'd fallen!"

Smashie thought better of mentioning that she had, indeed, clonked her head.

"Can't say I'm not glad to be staying on my bus for the duration of this trip," murmured Mr. Potter. "Got a good novel to read and a nice bottle of iced tea."

"It's clear I am doing a terrible job watching Smashie today," said Grammy.

"I bet you could use a break," said Mr. Bloom. "Why, I'd be glad to spend the day with Miss McP. Make sure she don't get into any more mischief. And Ms. Early, while we're at it, why don't you give me Mr. M. as well?"

"Dontel?" asked Ms. Early. "But he's been so well behaved—oh." She broke off. "Certainly you may take him as well, as long as it's all right with his grandmother."

"It's fine with me," said Mrs. Marquise.

"Then come along," said Mr. Bloom to Smashie. If she didn't know better, she'd've thought his tone suggested that he had a plan himself.

CHAPTER 28

Reconciliation and A Star Is Born!

Room 11 went into the planetarium as a body. Only three people hung back. Smashie, Mr. Bloom, and Dontel.

"Why do you want me, too, Mr. Bloom?" asked Dontel. "I've been good! *I* didn't dangle!"

"Because you two need to talk," said Mr. Bloom. "And I'm going to get out of the way and let you do it. We'll be right with you all!" he called to Ms. Early, as their docent, a kindly, excitable young man with a clipboard in his hands, directed Room 11 to put its backpacks down in a neat pile by a sign that read:

WELCOME TO THE STEPHEN HAWKING PLANETARIUM!

- *The heads of planetariums meeting is down the hall in the Niels Bohr Lounge.*

- *The children's Space Project Contest is in the adjacent Ada Lovelace Conference Room.*

- *The planetarium show will be held in the Mae Jemison Theater.*

Mr. Bloom looked at the two quarreling children. "I'll back up a few steps," he said. "Let you have some privacy." And he turned his back to them to look at a picture of the moon hanging on the wall.

Smashie gulped.

Dontel swallowed.

"Dontel—I—"

"Smashie, you—"

"Let's not talk at the same time," said Smashie. "Do you want to go first, or do you want me to?"

"You can go," said Dontel. He made as if to fold his arms across his chest but dropped them listlessly by his sides instead.

Maybe he was as sad about fighting as she was, thought Smashie.

She gulped again. "Dontel, I had no right to take your drawing without permission. I was wrong, and I am well and truly sorry and will do everything I can to either find it or help you make a new technically correct drawing of a space rocket."

Dontel looked at her. Then he smiled a tiny smile. "Smashie," he said, "I forgive you."

Smashie burst into tears.

"I even did dangling to try to find your drawing," she said, sobbing.

"I know," said Dontel. "Please don't cry, Smashie," he pleaded. "I've been feeling awful. Why, of course I should have forgiven you right away! You're my best friend, and I know you only had my best interests at heart when you stole—took—whatever—*had* my drawing. My parents and grandma always talk about forgiving people, and I should have forgiven you way sooner." He shook his head. "It was an awful bus ride, being in a fight with you."

Smashie's sobs had become gulps, and now they stopped. "Dontel," she said, "thank you. You are my favorite person in the world outside of my own family, and I was devastated that you might not like me anymore."

"Never," said Dontel, patting her on the shoulder. "I could never stay mad at you forever."

"I wasn't sure," said Smashie.

"I was," said Mr. Bloom, coming up to them from the discreet position he had taken behind them. "And now that you two are friends again, suppose we go join the group."

"I could be your assistant on the new technically correct drawing of a space rocket if our investigation doesn't work and we can't find out what happened to the old one," Smashie said eagerly as she bounced along beside Dontel on their way toward their class. "I can hand you the cards where you wrote your research! Pass you the special colors of pen you need for each part of the rocket!"

"Thanks, Smash," said Dontel. "And I bet you'd have a lot of other good ideas, too. We are a good team when we work together."

And the two friends exchanged beams as they reached the cluster of Room 11, its chaperones, and the young docent with the clipboard.

"Speaking of investigations," whispered Smashie, "guess what I found when I was dangling on the bus?"

"Shh," said Dontel. "I think this man needs to talk to us."

"But I have too much to tell you! Dontel, it was the missing space-related snack I found! It was under Willette's seat! We have to tax her! Even though taxing doesn't always go so well. But what I can't make out is her motive. Did she want all the cookies for herself? Nobody could eat all those space-related snacks. Maybe she was worried about our health. But a cookie every once in a while can't hurt you. Why, I think—"

But she was interrupted by the docent.

"My name is Jim," said the docent, who was tall and thin as a willow. "And I'll be leading you through the exhibits today before we see the planetarium show. You should feel free to stop and ask me questions at any time. There are a lot of terrific things for us to see and do, so we better get started!"

He led them to the first exhibit, which was called *You Spin Me Right Round, Baby!* and was all about far-away galaxies.

"You're to express the life cycle of a galaxy through interpretive dance!" cried the docent. "Does dancing make you feel shy?"

"No," the children reassured him, glancing at Smashie. "We have dance experience."

Billy was already swooping his arms about. "I

want to be a galaxy with tentacle arms," he said.

"I'm going to use these ribbons to swirl like intergalactic membranes!" Charlene shouted.

The dancing ended all too soon and they entered the next exhibit. It was called *Great Balls of Fire!* and was about the nature of the sun. Here, the children played heat-sensing molecules in a huge solar thermometer to understand how the heat of the sun could be measured.

"Now I get why molecules are far apart from each other when they're heated!" said Joyce.

"Yeah! They want to spread out!"

"Like us when it's hot outside!"

"No huddling up like we do when it's cold!"

The exhibits and activities were wonderful, but, frustratingly, Mr. Bloom stayed true to his promise and stuck to Smashie and Dontel like glue throughout so they were not able to exchange a single word about any of their investigations.

Not about the space-related snack and certainly not about the disappearance of Dontel's drawing of a technically correct space rocket.

Now they were in what was to be the final exhibit of the day before the planetarium show and it looked to be the most beautiful of all. "Welcome to our *A Star Is Born!* exhibit," said Jim the docent. "Take a nice first look around from here." He gestured at the beautiful space photographs that hung all around the room of the exhibit hall. The pictures were glorious—full of plumes of fluorescent-colored gases with bright lights twinkling inside them everywhere.

"Take good notes in here, children," said Ms. Early. "There will be a lot of information that we can use when we get back to school and start working on our unit."

"May we get our notebooks back out of our backpacks?" asked Joyce.

"Certainly," said Ms. Early, and there was a mad scramble to the pile of backpacks near the entrance to the exhibits. Except for Smashie and Dontel.

"I still have my Investigation Notebook with me," said Smashie, pulling it out of the sash she had made of Jacinda's scarf. Joyce's mother's large flappy gloves were awfully hot, so she took them off and tucked them into the scarf. The scarf would have to be suit enough.

"I do, too," said Dontel, and he pulled his notebook out of the capacious pocket of his Rebecca Lee Crumpler hoodie.

The two friends beamed. For they knew, although they would listen closely to what Jim the docent had to teach them, they would also try to use this time to do some much needed investigating.

Jim the docent addressed the group. "In a way, you can think of nebulae as being nurseries for baby stars. Gravity makes dust and gases coagulate inside them until there's enough of it to turn into stars and even some baby planets. Why don't you take a look at the pictures," he said, "and then we'll come back together to talk some more about it?"

"Swell!" cried Room 11, and hurried to the first picture in the exhibit.

"New planets," Mr. Bloom muttered next to Smashie and Dontel. "That means possible new alien life-forms." And, completely forgetting his two charges, he hurried to the first picture with the rest of Room 11 for a good look at the baby planets' environs.

"We're free!" cried Smashie. "This is our chance to share what we each learned on the bus for our investigations!"

"Yes," Dontel agreed. "I still want to see these pictures, though, and we don't want to get into trouble. So why don't we talk as we go from picture to picture? But since the whole class is starting at the first picture and going around to the last, let's start at the *last* one and go backward to the first one," he suggested. "That way we'll have more privacy to discuss clues."

"Should we talk about the mystery of the space-related snack first?" asked Smashie. "To get it out of the way? I guess it's solved. I mean, Willette had the cookies right under her seat."

"But I don't understand how she had them if they were found first up by my grandma's feet," admitted Dontel. They paused for a moment to look at a huge photograph of the Horsehead Nebula. "Should we tax Willette?"

Smashie beamed at the thought. Then her smile faded. "I don't see how we can tax Willette here in the exhibit hall. It hasn't gone so well when we've taxed people publicly before. Even today," she said, remembering Tatiana. "Besides," she said slowly, "I am getting another idea."

They headed to the next-to-last picture as their classmates began to move interestedly from picture to picture in the other direction.

"Check out this one, John!"

"Take a look at this, Willette!"

"Ahoy The Haddock!" Joyce said, and bumped fists with Charlene.

"Why people like that The Haddock, I will never understand," sighed Dontel.

"Me, either," said Smashie, glad they were able to agree on this together again at last. "Brainyon says: Use your brains!" she called.

And she and Dontel bumped fists, too. John gave them a thumbs-up from his position in the group of children.

"But what I don't get either is what you said

before," Dontel said. "The motive. It's just not strong enough. And stealing the snack is rude to our grandmas, too, when they took so much trouble to make that snack with us for the class. Why, the kids were even rudish to them when our grandmothers were investigating the case. Kept saying they should stop."

"That was only a compliment to us, though," said Smashie. "Room 11 believes in our skill as investigators."

She paused significantly.

"What, Smashie?"

"Think about it. They didn't wanted our grandmothers to investigate. Only us."

Dontel stared at her. "What do you mean?"

"Why aren't you two going around the exhibit with your classmates?" Jim the docent had appeared beside them, smiling.

"Yargh!" Smashie could not resist a cry of frustration. Here she was, on the edge of cracking at least one of the cases, and another adult had come to thwart their conversation!

"We just . . . we just really like that picture of the

Horsehead Nebula," said Dontel hastily to cover Smashie's cry. "It's in the Orion constellation, and that's one of my favorites."

The docent beamed. "Why, you know a lot about astronomy already, don't you? That's great!"

Dontel looked down shyly. "I love it," he said. "My grandmother and I talk about it all the time. She's one of our chaperones today." Dontel nodded in his grandma's direction. "I read a lot about it, too."

"Well, you sound like a born astrophysicist," said Jim. "If you love astronomy that much, stick with it. That's what I did. I'm learning to be an astrophysicist right now."

"You are?" Smashie and Dontel looked up at the docent in awe.

"Sure," he said. "I'm in college and that's my major. It's why I love being a docent here in the planetarium as well. I get to be surrounded by stuff about the universe all the time!"

Dontel gulped. "That's my dream, too," he said.

"Then stay with it and never give up. No matter what," said Jim. He peered at Dontel's name tag. "Dontel Marquise. That sounds like a good name for a future head of a planetarium."

Smashie beamed. "That's what I think, too!"

"Tell you what, Dontel," said the docent. "I'll give you and your grandmother my contact information. And if you ever want any advice about studying astrophysics, or college, or summer space camps or even just encouragement—why, you just get in touch with me and I'd be happy to help you."

"Really?" Dontel looked at the docent as if he were a rock star and had just pulled Dontel onto the stage to dance with the band. "I'd be very grateful for that."

"Consider it done," said the docent. "But here comes the rest of your class. It's time to go to the planetarium show. You're going to love it if you love Orion. The show has a ton of wonderful information about constellations!"

Dontel smiled, then gave a start.

"Smashie," he whispered to her as the docent returned to the main body of the group. "You know what's even better than a constellation? A SUSPECT!"

CHAPTER 29

The Planetarium Show

"A suspect?" cried Smashie. "Do you mean in the cookies mystery?"

"No!" said Dontel. "I mean in the mystery of the disappearance of my technically correct space rocket plans! Who," he asked, "also has an interest in space?"

"Mr. Bloom?" said Smashie incredulously. "Dontel, I don't think—"

"Not Mr. Bloom," said Dontel. "Of course I don't

mean him. But who was a little mad that we got to go to Mr. Bloom's trailer this morning when the kids volunteered us to go pick up the materials because we love astronomy best?"

"I don't know," admitted Smashie. "A couple of the kids were muttering about that before they came around."

"Well, what Jim the docent said just now reminded me. Which child said he'd been to *space camp?*" asked Dontel.

Smashie gasped. "Not John! Oh, why do we keep having to suspect our closest friends? And why in the world would *John* steal your drawing?"

Dontel flipped open his Investigation Notebook. It was clear he had been working as hard as Smashie on the case when they had been fighting. He turned now to his Motives List and thumped it with his hand.

2. Someone loves space stuff but wants to be the first one in Room 11 to build a rocket and hasn't learned enough about it yet.

3. Someone loves space stuff and wants to build the rocket himself or herself at home for the sheer fun of it.

"I guess both of those could fit John, sort of," said Smashie slowly. "But, Dontel—"

"We're taxing John," said Dontel firmly as the class formed a line to enter the planetarium show.

"Taxing me about what?" asked John. He was right behind them in line.

"About my drawing," said Dontel.

"You think I had something to do with that?" said John in disbelief. "You're bugging, man."

"But you love space," said Smashie weakly. "You went to space camp."

"You think going to space camp makes a person a thief? Thanks a lot, guys. I'm going to go back and stand with Alonso."

And he did.

"Taxing never goes well for us," said Dontel miserably. "I don't know whether that exonerates John or not."

"Well, I believe him," said Smashie. "His feelings really did seem hurt."

"Why do we always mess up so much while we solve mysteries?" Dontel said with a sigh. "I've been looking forward to this planetarium show for weeks, and now I don't know if I'll be able to enjoy it at all," he said to Smashie as Room 11 filed excitedly into the theater at last.

"I know," said Smashie. "I'm just wishing we could get back on that bus and do some more investigating."

"You haven't even told me what you mean about the cookies yet, either," Dontel reminded her. He sat down on Smashie's right. Jacinda was on her left. The planetarium seats were extremely comfortable—puffy and soft, with large armrests. Room 11 and its chaperones wiggled happily into position.

"Maybe we'll have a chance to talk during the film," said Smashie hopefully. "It will be dark in here and people will be watching the show."

"I'm sure I don't need to remind you that there is absolutely no talking during this film," said Ms.

Early, standing in front of her class.

"Darn," said Smashie.

"WELCOME!" boomed a voice from the speakers. "THE STEPHEN HAWKING PLANETARIUM IS HONORED TO PRESENT TO YOU OUR SPACE SHOW, ENTITLED *BEHOLD THE NIGHT SKY!*"

"That voice is awfully loud," whispered Dontel to Smashie.

"Just the way I like it," Smashie whispered back. "Ms. Early won't hear us talking, so we maybe we can investigate in here after all!"

"In this theater," the narrator continued through the speakers, "we don't look forward at a screen. Rather, we look up. Your seats will now tip back so you can see the screen that stretches across the dome of our ceiling."

There was a mechanical whirl, and then Smashie felt her seat tip backward, so she was practically lying down, as if her chair had become a chaise longue.

"Oooh!"

"Neat!"

"This is something!"

Everybody was excited, even the adults.

Dontel nudged Smashie. "Look up!"

And Smashie did. The ceiling dome was dark as the night sky, covered in stars, a big swath of them forming a gorgeous thick line across the highest arc of the dome.

"This is the Milky Way. Our galaxy," boomed the narrator. The film zoomed in on the galaxy until it showed a familiar image of eight planets circling around a star. "And our solar system is at one of the Milky Way's outer edges, revolving around our star, the sun. But we can't see the sun in our night sky." The sun winked out, leaving the images of many new stars in its wake. "What we *can* see are other stars. We are now looking at the same stars seen by people all over the Northern Hemisphere, the very same stars our ancestors saw. And virtually every culture in the world has told stories about the stars they see," the narrator continued. "We'll begin with some of the stories from the Greeks, whose many myths are illustrated by the way they saw these stars in the night sky. The clusters of stars that they made into pictures are called constellations. The first one we'll look at is Orion the hunter, standing tall with a sword hanging from his belt."

Dontel squirmed. Smashie knew that, as wonderful as it was to be lying down to watch a show about his favorite subject and constellation, even, he was itching to get back to the investigation. Where was his drawing? Was John really innocent? Was Tatiana? Would they ever find the drawing at all? All that work! Re-creating the drawing would take forever! Maybe they wouldn't even be done with it before the unit was over! Maybe they wouldn't even get to make the rocket and take it out on the athletic fields to let her rip! Maybe—

"And here," continued the narrator, "is the constellation Cassiopeia, shaped like the letter *W*."

"Well, I know someone who looks like the letter *A*." The whisper came from Jacinda's head, snapping toward Smashie from the left.

"What are you talking about?" whispered Smashie back indignantly, snapping her own head to the side to look at Jacinda. "I do not look like the letter *A*!"

"Not your *person*," said Jacinda. "But you look like someone whose name starts with *A*."

Smashie sat bolt upright. "What do you mean, Jacinda?"

"Quiet, Smashie!"

"Sorry, Grammy!" Smashie subsided back into her chair, but with her head still facing Jacinda, rather than the ceiling.

"What do you mean, Jacinda?" she said again, but this time in a whisper.

"I mean this, Smashie McPerter!" whispered Jacinda back. "I know your initials are AAM!"

"They are not!" said Smashie, uncomfortable. "Why do you even think that? My last initial is special because it's a McSomething name, remember? That's why Mr. Bloom calls me Miss McP.!"

"Tchah!" said Jacinda. "Your Grammy embroidered AAM on your homburg. We all saw when we were playing with your hats."

"That's what I'm saying," said Smashie. "It doesn't end in McP.!"

"*That's only because your grammy can't embroider*

curved lines yet! I heard her tell Dontel's grandma,"
Jacinda hissed. "That's why she couldn't embroider
the little *c* and the capital *P* for AAMcP! They have
curved lines in them! So she had to stop at the *M*. That
means the *A* and the other *A* stand for your real given
names!"

Smashie slouched as low as she could in her chair.
This was terrible.

"Why did I ever teach you how to investigate?"
she said miserably.

"Quiet down there!" Mr. Bloom's voice was not
pleased.

But Jacinda was undeterred. "I'm right, aren't I?!"
Her whisper was triumphant.

Smashie looked down at her planetarium-raised
knees. "Why are you being so mean?" she whispered
to Jacinda. "I thought we were good friends!"

"Oh, we are!" said Jacinda. "I really like you! It's
just that I am so curious about your name. What
could it be?"

"Let us turn now to the constellations represent-
ing the signs of the zodiac," the narrator was saying

now. "We begin with Aquarius, the water bearer—"

"Aquarius!" whispered Jacinda to Smashie. "Is your name Aquarius?"

"No," whispered Smashie. "Don't be ridiculous!"

"The protector of the constellation Aries is Athena, goddess of wisdom and the arts—" the narrator went on.

"Aries!" Jacinda's head snapped back toward Smashie. "Your name is Aries Athena! Or Athena Aries!"

"It is *not!*"

"Artemis, the goddess of the hunt," continued the narrator, "protects the constellation Sagittarius, the archer. Like Artemis and Orion, Sagittarius was a hunter—"

"Is your name Artemis?" asked Jacinda. "It is, isn't it? I've guessed it!"

"No!" said Smashie, tortured. "Please quit guessing!"

"If you kids don't pipe down, down there, I'm going to have to come march you up to sit with the adults," boomed Grammy.

Dontel nudged Smashie quiet, though his eyes were questioning.

Smashie subsided.

So did Jacinda. She looked straight up at the ceiling. But Smashie knew Jacinda would never give up, not until she knew Smashie's given name.

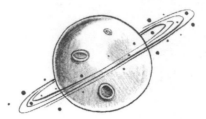

CHAPTER 30

Emergency Meeting

Room 11 left the planetarium, popping with ideas.

"Ms. Early, we could invent planets based on what we learned about how they form and we could write about them, too!"

"And then we could imagine alien creatures that live on them!"

"Don't have to imagine about that," muttered Mr. Bloom.

"Ms. Early, could we turn our whole classroom

into a planetarium and invite our families to a planetarium show kind of like what we just saw, only with what we learn?"

"These are all very, very fine ideas," said Ms. Early warmly. "I think we can do them all. As well as read and read and write and write about space and the universe."

"Hooray!" cheered Room 11.

"But I'm afraid I am not at all happy with all the whispering that went on in that planetarium show, especially after I had expressly told you there was no talking allowed. Smashie McPerter—"

"Andromeda Apollo," muttered Jacinda.

"You whispered and chattered and nearly shouted. What was the matter with you, that you were being so disrespectful?"

"I'm sorry, Ms. Early. I'm sorry, Room 11. I—"

But they were interrupted. Jim the docent had spotted them leaving the theater and now he was running toward them at top speed.

"Rebecca Lee Crumpler, Room 11?" he puffed as he reached them. "You're wanted right away in the Ada Lovelace Conference Room!"

"We are?" Ms. Early was startled. "But we didn't plan an activity there—"

"I'm sorry to hurry you, but my boss said to have you come quick. It's something wonderful."

"The Ada Lovelace Conference Room is right next to the Niels Bohr Lounge, where the heads of planetariums are meeting!" said Dontel to Smashie, grabbing her arm. "Do you realize there will be just a thin wall separating us from Dr. Bryson's best friend?"

"Yes!" said Smashie. "Maybe we can sit along that wall and press our ears against it and listen in! You could hear Dr. Bryson's best friend's actual voice, in person!"

Dontel gulped at the thought.

Room 11 hustled into the conference room. They were not the only children there. Visitors from other elementary schools stuffed the room to its gills. Like Room 11, they were mostly dressed in matching sweatshirts with school logos. At the front of the room there were large tables, covered with dioramas, models, and all manner of reports in colorful folders.

The door opened, and several adults came in—including Dr. Alison Subramanian, head of the M. W. Teck Observatory in Hawaii.

Dr. Subramanian.

Cornelius DuVasse Bryson's best friend.

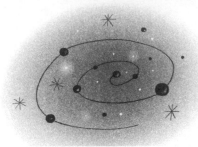

CHAPTER 31

Heads of Planetariums

Dontel gawked at her. He gaped.

"Dontel," whispered Smashie. "Close your mouth. You don't want to look like The Haddock."

Dontel closed his mouth immediately and assumed an expression of intelligence worthy of Brainyon.

"Children," said Dr. Subramanian, "as part of our meeting today, my colleagues and I have had the honor of judging the space projects some of you entered in to this planetarium's contest. And, while we've had a hard time of it, we've finally narrowed it down to the top three projects."

One of the other heads of planetariums who had entered the room with Dr. Bryson's best friend spoke next. "The winner and first two runners-up of the contest will receive special pins admitting them to the Junior Astrophysicists Society of the United States," he told them, and the room burst into applause. "And," he continued, "the first-place winner shall also have the opportunity to lunch with his or her choice of one of the heads of planetariums who is here today."

Smashie looked at Dontel. He looked crestfallen. She knew he was regretting his choice not to enter the contest.

His grandma knew, too. "Be a good sport," she whispered to him now. "We have to be happy for the children who will win."

"I know." Dontel nodded. "I will be. And the next time, maybe I'll be brave enough to enter my work."

"That's my boy," his grandma said, and hugged his shoulders.

"Second runner-up goes to Lily Podkopayeva

from the Penelope Fitzgerald Elementary School, for her beautiful diorama of Mars and the Mars rover!" said Dr. Subramanian. "Let's give it up for Lily!"

Everybody clapped as Lily from the Penelope Fitzgerald Elementary School went up and received her pin.

"Sure is shiny," whispered Dontel sadly. Smashie patted his arm as said Dr. Alison Subramanian spoke again.

"First runner-up goes to Simona Byle from the Leonardo da Vinci School for Science and the Arts for her wonderful model alien robot with movable legs. Let's hear it for Simona!"

Everybody clapped, Dontel hardest of all. "That's amazing!" he whispered to Smashie and his grandma. "Why, I'd love to learn how to do that. What great projects these kids made!"

"That's my boy," his grandma said again, and hugged his shoulders even closer.

"And in first place, a truly marvelous project," said one of the other heads of planetariums. "One that impressed us all."

"Our decision was unanimous," said Dr. Alison Subramanian herself. "This is a project marked for its research, care, love for its subject, and plain hard work. First place goes to Dontel Marquise from the Rebecca Lee Crumpler Elementary School for his technically correct plans for a real space rocket!"

Room 11 and its chaperones erupted in applause and squeals and hoots.

Smashie nudged Dontel. "Dontel," she said, "you won! Go up there!"

"But how could I win if I didn't even enter?"

"I don't know," said Smashie and Mrs. Marquise at the same time.

"But don't knock it and get up there!" Smashie added.

And Dontel moved to the front of the room as if on borrowed legs.

"Mr. Marquise," said Dr. Subramanian, bending to shake Dontel's hand. "How did you learn so much about the mechanics of building a rocket?"

"I . . . I . . ." Dontel struggled to overcome his shyness from being in front of the best friend of the man he looked up to most, second only to his own father. "I read a lot of books and tested a lot of ideas until I came up with something that would work. Me and my class—that's Room 11 over there in the red hoodies—our teacher said we could build it during our astronomy unit."

"I'm pleased to hear that you were so thoughtful with your work," said Dr. Bryson's best friend. "And I'd love to be there when you let her rip. May I come visit that day?"

"YES!" cried Room 11, Ms. Early, and the chaperones.

"Then you and I can have lunch after!" said Dontel. "You are who I pick! Please? I'd love to eat with you and ask you questions about the universe, if you don't mind."

"I don't mind at all!" said Dr. Subramanian.

"Maybe you could write up her answers for the school paper," suggested Charlene, her eyes shining with pride for Dontel.

Dontel nodded. Smashie knew he was too moved to speak anymore. But he gulped once,

then swallowed and addressed Dr. Bryson's best friend once more. "Thank you very much, Dr. Subramanian. And all of you judges. I guess this is maybe the best day of my life."

"Mine, too," said Smashie. Grammy patted Smashie on the hand.

"That's my girl," she said.

The room began to break up as the children from other schools followed their teachers out of the room.

"Line up, Room 11!" called Ms. Early. "Time to go! Let's thank all the heads of planetariums for making our trip so special."

"Thank you!" chorused Room 11, and they made to leave the room.

"Wait!" It was Jim the docent. He pumped Dontel's hand, then Ms. Early's. "I am so proud of you," he said to Dontel. "And I meant it about staying in touch. Here's my card." And he handed a card with his email address and phone number to Mrs. Marquise. "I'd be happy to help Dontel with anything to do with our mutual love of the universe."

"Who could not love the universe?" wondered Dontel. "It's so beautiful."

"Hear, hear," said the grandmothers, and Room 11 filed out of the room at last.

Smashie hugged Dontel. "I'm so proud of you, too," she said. "But now we have to finish solving all these mysteries. Never mind this new one of how your picture got entered into the contest without you knowing!"

"Mr. Marquise!" It was Dr. Subramanian. The whole class stopped and turned around to look at her in awe. "One last thing. This was on the tube containing your drawing. Almost as if in triumph over it, with a fishy foot on the lid." And she held out an action figure of The Haddock. "I mean, from my point of view, yours is much more of a Brainyon rocket," she said. "But if you love The Haddock, then—"

"I do not love The Haddock," said Dontel flatly. "But I know someone who does." Then he turned to look at Smashie. Light dawned in his eyes. "Wait a minute."

"Yep," said Smashie. "Clonk, clonk. I think we are going to have a heck of a postmortem on that bus, Dontel. And I know just what hat I'm going to wear, too!"

"And I," said Dontel, "would be proud to wear that mustache."

Smashie nearly died of joy. Dontel would be in something of a suit at last.

CHAPTER 32

Postmortem

The children were on the bus. Dr. Subramanian had shaken everyone's hand and made plans with Ms. Early to come to the school the day the rocket was finished to watch its launch and to have the special lunch with Dontel. Except for Billy, who had had his The Haddock confiscated by Ms. Early again, delight was the order of the day as the children took their seats.

But it didn't last long for Smashie. "We forgot about my turban!" she exclaimed. "It's still missing!"

"Here, let's look around under the seats," said Tatiana.

"Don't bother," said Dontel, who had come down the bus aisle behind Smashie. "I think I have an idea where that turban might be."

"Where?" asked Joyce and Jacinda in unison.

But Dontel said nothing. He only gave Smashie a speaking look.

Smashie turned to Mr. Bloom.

"Mr. Bloom," she said, "do you mind if I go up and sit with Dontel again? We have a lot to discuss."

"I betcha do," said Mr. Bloom. "I don't mind at all."

"Thank you," said Smashie. "And I really enjoyed spending time with you today. Even if it was because I was dangling and planning to break rules three, four and five and you had to keep an eye on me."

"My pleasure, Miss McP. At least you didn't break rule number two with me."

"Miss McP., ha!" Jacinda opened her mouth to continue, but Smashie cut her off.

"Jacinda! Please!" she cried.

"Argh!" said Jacinda. "Why not?"

"Because it embarrasses me!" Smashie said, and she hurried up the aisle away from Jacinda and her knowledge and toward Dontel and his.

The bus had not yet started. Mr. Potter was outside with Cyrus and Grammy, looking at the rigged-up tailpipe to make sure everything looked okay back there before they started back to the school.

"Let's compare notes," whispered Dontel as Smashie sat down beside him.

"I've been waiting all day for this!" whispered Smashie back.

And they spoke even more quietly.

". . . clonk . . . enthusiasm . . . Haddock . . . John . . . tube . . . Tatiana . . ." were the only words that could be heard from their seat.

"Have we got it all sorted out?" asked Dontel at last, sitting straight up and closing his Investigation Notebook.

"We do," said Smashie, sitting up and doing the same.

"Then," said Dontel, "may I please have that mustache?"

"Certainly," said Smashie, handing it over with

tremendous pride for her friend. She fished about in her backpack and came up with a small tube. "And here is some spirit gum to stick it on with."

"Thank you," said Dontel.

"I don't really want to wear my homburg for the postmortem," said Smashie, mindful of the AAM embroidered on the side. She didn't want anyone else besides Jacinda getting ideas about her name. "But that Russian one is too hot and covers my whole face, anyway." And so she took the homburg and set it on her head.

"Don't worry," said Dontel. "You look great, like a real gumshoe."

"That's just what Grammy said!" Smashie cried. But she grew quiet once more and looked at her friend. "Dontel," said Smashie, "it's time."

"Yes," agreed Dontel. "I think it is."

"Only I think we need to pace purposefully back and forth for this," said Smashie.

"I do, too," said Dontel. "Let's get in the aisle."

And both of them moved out of their seat into the aisle. Smashie paced toward the front of the bus. Dontel paced toward the back.

"What is going on here?"

Smashie collided with Grammy, who had just climbed back on the bus with Cyrus and Mr. Potter.

"We're going to have a postmortem, Grammy. Go over all the mysteries and figure out the whodunit part."

"Oooh!" said Grammy. "I'm always up for a good postmortem. Though I'm afraid Mrs. Marquise and I don't have much to offer. We only found those cookies by accident. And then they disappeared again."

"Maybe, Sue, if you hadn't been so shouty with our clues—"

"Now, Lorraine—"

"Is this postmortem thing going to last a long time?" interrupted Mr. Potter wearily. "Because it's almost time for me to get off work."

"It will not," said Ms. Early after she had counted to make sure all of the children were safely on the bus. "Smashie and Dontel, I am going to allow this postmortem, but only because I am as curious as you are as to how Dontel's drawing went missing and then turned up in the contest to win the whole thing! What all is going on?"

Smashie and Dontel continued to pace.

"It all started when our grandmothers came into the classroom this morning," Smashie began. "Well, I guess it actually started last night, when we baked and frosted the cookies for the space-related snack. Cookies that you will find"—she whipped her head around to the back of the bus—"under the seat of Willette Williams right now."

"Willette!" Ms. Early was shocked.

Smashie put up a cautionary hand. "It isn't what you think, Ms. Early. The cookie theft was made to look nefarious, but it was not."

"What are you even talking about?" asked Charlene. There were curious looks, lips being bitten, and eye slides going on all over the bus.

Dontel stroked his pretend mustache. "Let's not discuss the space-related snack just yet. Let's start, instead, with the other mystery—the disappearance of my technically correct plans for a space rocket. In this case," he continued, pacing slowly up the aisle, "there is an easy explanation for the disappearance of my drawing and its turning up in the contest—and a

complex one. We will start"—he whirled around—"with the complex one."

"I think it just rolled off the bus when we were at the rest stop," said Alonso. "I think a teacher from another school found it and recognized it as a child's space project and put it in the contest pile when their school got to the museum and then Billy snuck his The Haddock onto it when we were called into the room by Jim the docent."

"That," said Smashie, holding on to her homburg, "would be the easy explanation."

"Really?" asked Ms. Early.

"Yes," said Smashie firmly. "But as Dontel says, let's begin with the complex one."

"Our first clue came on the bus," said Dontel. "My drawing had gone missing, but you all wanted us to work the case of the missing, space-related snack instead."

"Why was that? we wondered," Smashie continued. "Why us, especially when there were already two crack detectives on the case? Adults, even?"

Both grandmothers bowed their heads slightly.

"Those people kept trying to foist the case on *us*," said Dontel, "and trying to foist our grandmothers *off* of it. It made no sense."

"Unless," said Smashie, "*it was a dummy case to divert Dontel and me from investigating the mystery we really were worried about—Dontel's missing drawing!*"

The bus gasped. "A dummy case?" they cried.

"A dummy case," said Smashie. "You all, Dontel worked so hard on that drawing! What other case could ever divert us from that? And what could have happened to Dontel's drawing? The answer," she said, and the bus gave a start, "was me."

The bus relaxed.

"At first, anyway," said Smashie.

The bus tensed again.

"I took it," Smashie continued. "As you all know, because I confessed that I did. And that I lost it."

"But Smashie didn't lose it," said Dontel. "Not at all. Smashie was not responsible for the disappearance of the tube containing my technically correct drawing of a space rocket the second time. Or the third time. Or even"—he whipped around and pegged Room 11 with a look—"the fourth."

Everyone reared back.

"For that was the case," said Smashie. "Dontel's tube was taken not once, but four times."

"How do you know that?" asked Mr. Bloom.

"Well," said Dontel, "it was only after Smashie told me her solution to the cookie case just now when we finally could compare notes that I figured it out."

"You have a solution to the cookie case, Smashie?" said Mrs. Marquise.

"Yes," said Smashie. "I do." She began to pace afresh. "During the first part of the bus ride, our bus sustained a mechanical problem."

"Tailpipe," said Mr. Potter. "This going to go much longer? Because I can't stay unless I get over-time pay."

"We will go as fast as we can, Mr. Potter," promised Dontel.

"Yes," said Smashie. "Anyway, while we were

stopped and Mr. Potter, Cyrus, and Grammy were fixing the bus, Dontel and I fought and then I had to go back to sit with Mr. Bloom. And while I was back there, I kept hearing little noises."

"*Clonk!*" went Dontel helpfully.

Smashie nodded.

"Like that," she said. "*Clonk!* At first, I thought something was wrong with the bus. I wondered if Mr. Potter, my grammy, and Cyrus had missed something."

"Never," said Mr. Potter. "I know my bus."

"Exactly, Mr. Potter," said Smashie. "You do. Then I noticed something else. Every time there was a clonk, it was followed by someone calling out something enthusiastic about our field trip. *Clonk*—'yay for the planetarium!' *Clonk*—'I love this field trip!' That kind of thing. On and on. First"—now it was Smashie's turn to whip around, her Homburg askew—"it was John. Then"—she whipped around again—"it was Charlene." Whip. "Then Willette. But then, after we got back on the bus from the rest stop and started moving again, there was another clonk.

And this time, there was no enthusiastic expression about our field trip."

"So?" said Willette. "We can't be excited every minute."

"Perhaps not," said Smashie. "But that clonk told me something else. My grammy shouted right after that that the container with the missing space-related snack had smacked Mrs. Marquise in the sneakers. And I realized that's what all the clonks were—the sound of a plastic container hitting sneakered feet."

Everyone looked down at their laps.

"People were zooming the cookie container under the bus seats to one another with their feet, and the enthusiastic comments were the sign that the container had been received by its intended target each time."

"Smashie," said Alonso, "you are smart."

"Thank you, Alonso," said Smashie. "But it was with YOU that the plan went wrong!"

"Me?!" cried Alonso. "What do you mean?" He shrank down in his seat.

"You'll soon see," said Smashie.

"Yes," said Dontel, twirling one end of his mustache.

"Anyway, when we got to the planetarium, I was in trouble, because my grammy caught me dangling from one of the bus seats."

"DON'T ANY OF YOU EVER TRY THAT, EVER," cried the chaperones in unison.

"Smashie is lucky she didn't get hurt," said Ms. Early.

"That's because she is bad at feats of physical prowess," said Billy.

"*Billy,*" said the bus.

"It's okay," said Smashie. "It's true. But first, it is important to note that before my grammy caught me dangling and picked me up to plonk me in the aisle, I saw something. The missing space-related snack under Willette's seat."

The bus turned to look at Willette again.

"But I couldn't tell Dontel," said Smashie, "because we were fighting. And I couldn't tell Ms. Early or my grammy, because I was in trouble for dangling. I had to keep the information to myself."

"And there is more," said Dontel. "For we mustn't

pass lightly over a discussion of the rest stop. It has great bearing on this case."

"You look very French in that mustache, Dontel," said Smashie's grammy.

"More Belgian," said Mrs. Marquise, and both ladies laughed. "Go on, Dontel."

"Thank you," said Dontel. "Well, when we stopped at the rest stop, I was so sad about the fight with Smashie, I didn't feel like playing tag."

"I was sad, too," said Smashie.

Dontel nodded. "So I just stayed sitting at my picnic table. I was facing the bus, and I saw something interesting." He paused and looked slowly around at his classmates. "Someone was inside the bus, pacing up and down the aisle wearing Smashie's turban. A turban"—he paused—"that has since gone missing."

The bus cast its eyes down.

"And when Dontel told me that he saw that," said Smashie, "I knew the turbaned person had taken the cookie container from under Willette's seat and brought it up to their own."

"But I thought you said Willette had it now," said Ms. Early. "I'm confused."

"Oh, she does have it," said Smashie confidently. "Willette, will you please reach under your seat and show us what's there?"

Reluctantly, Willette bent down and when she came back up, a familiar plastic container was in her hands.

"See?" said Smashie while the bus filled with whispered reactions and gasps. "We're coming to that—don't worry."

"When Smashie and I compared notes just now," said Dontel, "I could have sworn the turbaned person was Willette. Because she was the one who went back onto the bus during the rest stop, supposedly for her thermos."

"But I knew that was a dodge," said Smashie. "The perps were counting on the fact that we are all dressed alike today and it's hard to tell people apart from a distance. Especially if they're wearing my turban. It's so big, it covers a child's whole head. So it wasn't Willette in that turban on the bus. The turbaned person was actually—Alonso."

"Me?!"

"You," said Dontel firmly. "That stuck backpack

of yours was a scam. You just wanted time on the bus alone to get those cookies and bring them up to your seat."

"Yes," said Smashie, eyes glued to Alonso. "But then you made a mistake, Alonso Day. You planted the frosting on the bus seat as a clue for Dontel to find—just like Charlene dropped those crumbs for us to find, by the way, on her way up to our seat when she said she wanted to sit there and watch my grammy do her needlepoint. But instead, our grandmothers found the frosting before we did. And, then, instead of holding the cookies in place with your feet, Alonso, you accidentally kicked them backward when the bus started and *that* was when they hit Dontel's grandma in the sneakers."

"So that's how I got hit in the sneakers with my own cookies!" said Mrs. Marquise.

"We couldn't figure that out for the life of us!" added Grammy.

"Yep," said Smashie. "And that was why there was no enthusiastic expression about the field trip after that clonk! Then there was panic. Not just from Alonso—but from all of you involved in the crime."

"What do you mean?" cried the bus.

"With the cookies found, there was no way to try to divert my and Smashie's attention away from the mystery of the missing technically correct drawing of a space rocket," said Dontel. "So you had to steal the cookies again to try to lure us to solve that crime. The new cookie thief had to be someone at the front of the bus, and, since he was the last one to get a cookie, it had to be John. Among other reasons," he added pointedly.

This time, there was not an exclaimed "Me?!" John merely looked at Dontel, who returned his look. Then he continued.

"Then John slid the cookies back to Willette, where she received them with an expression of enthusiasm, and that's where they've been ever since."

Smashie turned to Ms. Early. "Ms. Early, can we pass them around and eat them now? We have a whole other part of the postmortem to do."

"My bus," moaned Mr. Potter.

"I'll clean it again," said Smashie.

"I'll help," said Dontel.

"Thank you," said Smashie.

"No problem," said Dontel.

"If you eat them carefully and promise to clean the bus, I think it would be fine to pass the cookies around," said Ms. Early.

"We will," promised the class.

"Go on, Mr. M.," said Mr. Bloom. "What about your drawing?"

"Well," said Dontel as he resumed his pacing as the plastic container began to make its rounds of the bus, followed by a wave of munching, "when Smashie told me she had figured out that the kids were shouting stuff about the field trip when they got the cookies, I realized there was another set of shouts going on. Either for The Haddock"—he pegged Charlene and Billy with a look—"or for Brainyon." And he looked at John. "And I realized that my technically correct drawing of a space rocket had been passed from hand to hand in a similar but more careful way, and that, this time, the The Haddock and Brainyon phrases were the signals that the receiver had safely gotten my tube from the pass-off person."

There was a pause as Dontel let that sink in.

"We thought people were talking about Brainyon and The Haddock so much because Dontel had stirred things up this morning with his plans to have Brainyon in the cockpit of his space rocket," said Smashie. "But that wasn't it at all. Kids were just showing that they had gotten the tube."

"They *kicked* your tube from person to person?" Ms. Early was aghast.

"No," said Dontel. "This was a much more careful operation. And it dovetailed with the cookie thefts, too."

"Explain, Mr. M.," said Mr. Bloom. "And go slow. I want to make sure we understand all this."

"Well," said Dontel, "I went back and looked at the suspect list Smashie and I had made. We had written down Siggie, Willette, Billy, Cyrus, John, and Smashie herself on our lists. But then after . . . after . . ."

"After you guys fought," said Billy helpfully.

"Yes," Dontel admitted. "I realized there were two other people who had had the opportunity to be in our room alone with no one watching before we left on our trip."

"Who?" asked Grammy.

"John and Joyce," said Dontel. "They both went back into the classroom at recess, purportedly to get things they forgot."

John and Joyce cast their eyes down.

"But they weren't the ones who took my drawing," said Dontel.

"They weren't?" asked Mr. Bloom.

"No," said Smashie. "What they were doing was hiding the space-related snack in the reading corner and Mrs. Marquise's tote bag in the backpack pile!"

"But Siggie checked that reading corner," said Ms. Early. "I saw him myself."

"That's why we crossed him out on the list of suspects at first, Ms. Early. Willette, too," said Smashie. "Siggie checked the reading corner, just like Willette checked the meeting area. But Siggie was really just covering up the fact that the space-related snack was there in the reading corner, where John and Joyce hid it when they came in from recess on their trumped-up excuse! But don't blame Siggie, Ms. Early. He was just following orders. Orders that came"—Smashie's homburged head whipped around—"from the mastermind of this plot. Willette Williams, we accuse you of being a cunning mastermind of this whole shebang!"

"Me?!" cried Willette.

The bus gasped.

"Yes," said Smashie. "You."

Willette emitted a squeal.

Smashie continued. "We think that you went and got the snack from the reading corner when you pretended to forget your backpack after we first got on the bus."

"*And*"—Dontel paused—"that wasn't the only part of the plot. John *was* involved. Just not for the reasons I thought he might be. Same with Tatiana. She was wearing her NASA T-shirt today and when Smashie and I were talking just now, we thought she might have taken the tube, too. Smashie even taxed her."

"I know!" cried Tatiana. "It was awful! I was afraid to say a word!"

"Sorry, Tatiana," said Smashie.

"Yes," said Dontel. "We were wrong about you. When we figured out that John and Joyce had hidden the snack and the tote bag, we realized that Willette wanted *Billy* to find the tote bag. For two reasons. One"—he spun around to face Billy in his seat at the back of the bus—"to start off the cookie mystery and for him to be its prime suspect. And two, so that Billy would have ample chance to be in the backpack area to steal my drawing tube and put it in his own backpack!"

The bus buzzed with conversation. Dontel held up a hand to quell it. His mustache had come somewhat loose on one side, but he still cut an impressive figure. "There is one thing I don't understand, though," he said. "And that is how Billy knew the drawing would be in Smashie's backpack and not mine."

"I think I can explain that," said Smashie. "I think Billy just opened the first black Brainyon backpack he saw and there was your tube and he just assumed it was your backpack. Ours are identical, after all."

"Oh." Dontel looked rather disappointed. Billy shrugged and suppressed a grin.

"Sorry it's not more than that," said Smashie.

"That's okay," said Dontel. "Anyway, Willette wanted to be sure that Smashie and I suspected Billy,

and Billy alone, of the crimes, if it came to our finding a solution."

"And it worked," said Smashie. "But not for the
cookie mystery. For the one about Dontel's missing
technically correct plans for a space rocket. I sure was
onto Billy for that one, even when Dontel and I were
fighting. Mr. Bloom and Joyce and Jacinda were helping me investigate and I saw that Billy had a green
smudge on his thumb, just like me, from the still-wet
marker letters on Dontel's tube. Billy made up some
excuse about it being from one of Ms. Early's markers, but that would have been quite a coincidence. So
we went through Billy's belongings."

"And found his The Haddock action figure, I might
add," said Mr. Bloom. He patted himself down and
shook his head. "How did you get that action figure
off me?"

Billy said nothing. But his shining eyes spoke
volumes.

"May we get back to the case?" asked Dontel.

"Certainly," said the bus.

"Thank you," said Smashie. "Anyway, I believed
Billy's excuse at the time."

"And then," Dontel continued, "just now, when I figured out about the The Haddock and the Brainyon exclamations being signals that people had received my drawing, I traced those exclamations and I knew it went from Billy to John—"

"And then *back to Billy's backpack when we were at the rest stop*," Smashie concluded.

"But Billy couldn't have taken it back at the rest stop," Cyrus protested. "He didn't get back on the bus. He was talking to Tatiana the whole time."

"Exactly," said Dontel. "It was Alonso, that turbaned figure, who took the cookies *and also* moved the tube from John's backpack back to Billy's, knowing that, since it was searched once, it would be unlikely for it to be searched again."

The bus was silent, although Billy's face was chumped up with suppressed pride.

"So it was all a matter of who went where when with what," said Smashie.

The bus paused, admiring the sentence. Then it shook itself.

"Back to the case," said Grammy. "So it was Billy who snuck away to put your tube in that contest?"

"No," said Dontel. "Like we said, Billy was just the fall guy for the mysteries."

"What's a fall guy?" asked Siggie.

"It's someone who is set up to take the blame for a crime," Dontel explained. "Billy was the first one to take the tube, and the plan was to leave his signature, his The Haddock, on it at the museum so it would look like one of his pranks. At least that is what the culprits would have had us believe."

"That's Good Investigator Language," whispered Smashie. "Let's not forget to add *fall guy* to our list."

"Good idea," whispered Dontel. "Also *postmortem*."

But Mrs. Marquise was curious. "Please go on. Tell us who broke rules three, four, and five and snuck away from the group to hide your tube on the contest table. And *why*."

"If it wasn't Billy," Smashie began, but Ms. Early interrupted her.

"It wasn't," she said. "I can vouch for that. I had an eagle eye on Billy in that planetarium. He didn't disappear from my sight once."

"Aw, come on," said Billy.

Smashie nodded. "So someone else broke rules

three, four, and five and went and found that contest table and laid Dontel's tube down on it and filled out an entry form for the contest for it and, finally, took Billy's The Haddock and put it in a position of triumph on the top."

"That's pure me! No matter what anybody says!" Billy couldn't help himself. "I did that move the other week, remember?"

"I think you just like being the fall guy," said Dontel. "It wasn't you at all. Who it was, was"—and once more his head whipped around to the back of the bus—"Joyce."

"Joyce?" Ms. Early's voice was full of disbelief. "But Joyce is one of the kindest children in our class. I can't imagine she would break rules three, four, and five like that to play a trick on you."

"But she did," said Smashie. "In fact, we think Joyce is the cunning mastermind behind this whole plot!"

"I thought you said Willette was," said Charlene.

"We did," said Smashie. "It was the both of them, working together. We believe they got the idea to take Dontel's tube during morning meeting, when

Mrs. Marquise shared the drawing. The same time I got my idea to take it and present it to Dr. Bryson's best friend. But Willette and Joyce's plan was different. They wanted to take the drawing and sneak-enter it into that contest so Dontel would have a fair shot at winning, because he was too modest to do it himself."

"Why do you think it was us?" cried Willette and Joyce.

"Because we saw you whispering together at morning meeting," said Dontel. "And this is what shows how the complex the plan was. For it to involve so many kids passing my tube and the space-related snack, *all* of Room 11 must have been in on the plan. Willette, you and Joyce must have planned it with everybody at recess, when you sent us so firmly to Mr. Bloom's trailer. You wanted us out of the way so you could plan both the dummy mystery with the space-related snack, and the real one, the disappearance of my drawing and its entry into the contest. And you wanted Smashie out of the way because you thought she couldn't be trusted to keep a secret from me, on account of our being best friends. Though I guess"—Dontel's tone grew briefly hard—"you were wrong about that."

"Dontel," Smashie reminded him hastily, "you forgave me."

Dontel's shoulders relaxed. "I did." And he smiled at Smashie.

"Sneaking away from the group is a very serious offense, Joyce," said Ms. Early. "Even if your intentions to enter Dontel's work in that contest were good. Not everybody in the world is as nice as we are. It's important to stick with your class when we travel and not go wandering around on your own."

"It was only a short way down the hallway," said Smashie. "And easy for her to slip away—all the chaperones were as engrossed as the kids were by the pictures in the *A Star Is Born!* exhibit."

"That is true," said Ms. Early. "If Joyce snuck away, that is on me. I own it."

But Smashie and Dontel held up their hands.

"Wait, Ms. Early. There is more. There is still the small matter of my missing turban," asked Smashie. "Where did it go?"

"I'll tell you where," said Dontel. "What with our grandmothers investigating the cookies, the class was worried we'd be onto them about my drawing. They had to do something to distract us from any evidence of that theft. And that turban was a big piece of evidence, because whoever wore it took the cookies *and* moved the tube. I think you all were so worried about our figuring things out before the contest ended that someone took that turban and hid it."

"Where?" cried the bus.

"I have an idea." And Dontel unzipped his own backpack and pulled out the beautiful red satin turban, the jewel in its center gleaming.

The bus gasped.

"Joyce took it and pretended it was lost, then snuck

it into my backpack when she went to the backpack pile at the museum, so Smashie and I couldn't connect it to anyone else. Like Alonso."

He paused.

"So that is it. That's the complex explanation," said Dontel, his mustache now dangling rather rakishly over his upper lip. "Do we go with that? Because to do so would be to believe that all of Room 11 so believed in me and supported my work"—he gulped—"that they were willing to risk a whole lot of lying and breaking rules to see my drawing get a fair shot at winning that contest."

All around the bus, children gulped with him.

"Or," said Smashie, "do we go with the simple explanation? That Dontel's tube rolled off the bus when we were at the rest stop and a teacher from another school found it and recognized it as a child's space project and put it in the contest pile when their school got to the museum?"

The bus was silent.

"I'm moved, you guys," said Dontel. "And I thank you."

"We're moved, too," said Willette with a gulp.

"Let's go with the simple explanation!" cried Cyrus.

"Yes!"

"Let's!"

"That way no one is in trouble with the adults," said Billy practically.

"Dontel," said John, "Room 11 is very proud of you!"

"So are its chaperones!" said Mr. Bloom.

"And its bus driver, I gotta admit." Mr. Potter made as if to turn the key in the ignition. "But we really got to get going."

"There's just one more thing," said Jacinda. "It's time to talk about Smashie's homburg. And the letters embroidered on it."

CHAPTER 33

A Name

"Jacinda!" Smashie tried to clap her hands over the AAM embroidered on the side of the homburg. "How could you?"

"Smashie," said Jacinda firmly, "we all have wondered what your real name is ever since kindergarten. And obviously your grammy loves the name, or she would have embroidered an *S* instead of two *As* on the hat."

"No, I wouldn't have," said Grammy. "Can't embroider curved lines yet, remember? That's why it doesn't say SMcP like I wanted it to. I had to settle for the initials of Smashie's given name and just the *M* for her last name. I didn't mean to cause all this fuss about it, though. Her name really is her business."

"Hear, hear," said Ms. Early. "You all leave Smashie alone about it."

Smashie sighed. "Room 11, you all did so much for Dontel," she said. "Dr. Cornelius DuVasse Bryson's best friend is even coming to our school because of what you did. I guess you deserve something in exchange."

"Smashie, are you sure?" said Ms. Early.

The bus held its breath.

"Yes," said Smashie. "As long as everybody promises to keep it a Room 11 secret and never, ever calls me it as long as we live. Billy," she added pointedly.

"Why are you calling me out?" said Billy, but the familiar light died out of his eyes once again. "Oh, heck, fine," he said. "I owe you two."

"No, you don't," said Dontel. "You helped me win that contest and get the chance to shake Dr. Cornelius DuVasse Bryson's best friend's hand. I'll never forget it, Room 11. Not as long as I live."

Once again, the bus was full of moved snuffles.

"Back to Smashie's name," said Jacinda firmly.

"Well, do you all promise to agree to what I said?" Smashie asked her class.

"We promise," they solemnly vowed.

"My given name," said Smashie, "is Anna Anastacia."

CHAPTER 34

Smashie!

"That's a beautiful name!"

"I think that's real pretty."

"That's all it was the whole time? I thought it was going to be something like Frankenstein."

"Mrs. Tango," said Jacinda, "if Smashie has such a long and pretty name, why is she called Smashie?"

Grammy looked at Smashie. Smashie nodded back at her. It was okay for Grammy to tell the story.

"Well," Grammy began, "Anna Anastacia really is a long name for a baby to say. And Smashie couldn't say it. She called herself all kinds of things because she couldn't say Anna Anastacia. Tacie. Nacie. Sacie. And then at her first birthday party—"

"Which Dontel was at," Smashie reminded her grandmother.

Grammy nodded. "She smashed her fists into her birthday cake. And her mother said, 'No, Anna Anastacia! Don't smash your cake!' And Smashie just grinned and smashed her fists into her cake some more and cried, 'I Smashie! I Smashie!' So from then on, that's what we called her, too. It fit." Grammy sighed. "Smashie was a vigorous infant."

"Very," Mrs. Marquise confirmed.

"Thank you," said Jacinda. "And we will all keep our promise. You are Smashie for life."

"Here," said Joyce. "Have a cookie."

"Thank you," said Smashie. But as she moved to take the cookie, her homburg slipped over her eyes and she stumbled. The cookie immediately smashed into sticky bits in her hand.

"My bus!" moaned Mr. Potter.

"I Smashie!" said Billy, and Room 11 exploded in laughter. No one laughed harder than Smashie herself.

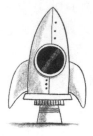

CHAPTER 35

Last of the Yayas

Smashie and Dontel were home at last. It was just before suppertime, and they sat on Dontel's porch steps, bundled in their coats, talking over the day and their argument and all the difficult mysteries they had been called on to solve.

"That was a lot of work," said Dontel.

"You said it," agreed Smashie. "And I did have to dangle to spy after all."

Dontel remained tactfully silent.

"You spied, too, if you think about it," said

Smashie. "You kept your eye on that bus and saw the turbaned figure, and that was a big key to our cracking the case. Isn't that what investigating is sometimes? Watching people who are behaving suspiciously and marking their movements to conquer injustice?"

"I guess," said Dontel. "All I know is that all that thinking and not giving up has given me a lot of yayas that I need to get out of my system before supper."

"Me too," said Smashie. "Let's run!"

And the two best friends ran around Dontel's yard like a couple of Brainyons in technically correct rockets shooting across the sky.

ACKNOWLEDGMENTS

I would like to thank the following people for their help and warm support while writing this book:

Allen K.
Tobin A.
Adrienne R.
Lizz Z.
Wendy B.
Ann C.
My beloved Alan G.
and, of course, the magnificent A. C.

DON'T MISS THE OTHER MYSTERIES STARRING
SMASHIE MCPERTER AND DONTEL MARQUISE!

Smashie McPerter
and the Mystery of Room 11

When Patches, the class pet, is stolen from Room 11, it turns out that a hamster heist is just the first mystery Smashie and her best friend, Dontel, must solve! Someone has also been gluing people to rulers and hats. As the peaceable and productive days of Room 11 turn into paranoia-fueled chaos, as natural suspects produce natural alibis and motives remain unmotivated, the two are determined to restore peace (and the hamster) before it's too late.

"Smashie's . . . positive energy
and determination are impressive."
—*Publishers Weekly*

"Well written and evenly paced, with great
supporting characters to root both for and against."
—*School Library Journal*

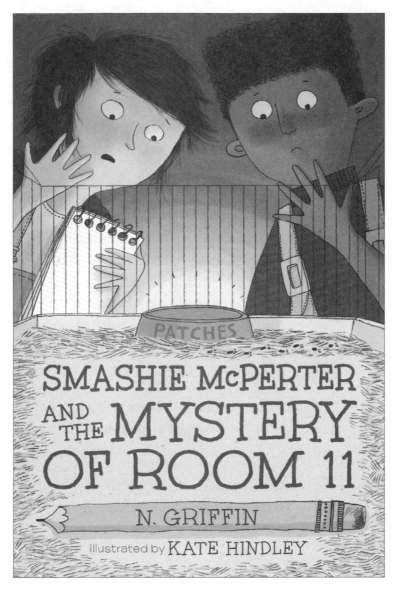

Available in hardcover and paperback and as an e-book

Smashie McPerter and the Mystery of the Missing Goop

There's never a dull moment in Room 11! When the third grade learns that they all must take part in a musicale, Smashie can't wait to sing something heartfelt and loud. But the others are not so eager. Luckily, Charlene's mom has agreed to donate her special gel that lengthens and sculpts hair into shapes (from a musical note to a roller skate), and soon all the kids are raring to go. That is, until their jars of goop go missing! Who would steal their beloved Herr Goop, and why? Time for Smashie and her best friend, Dontel, to get out their Investigation Notebooks!

"Griffin concocts a baroque plot involving
a secret code credibly based on third-grade
math and tells it with SAT-level vocabulary."

—*Kirkus Reviews*

"Smashie is still as vivacious and dramatic as when
readers last saw her, [and] Dontel is still his incredibly
patient and mature self. . . . The story is paced well, and
the plot is strong enough to intrigue a variety of readers."

—*School Library Journal*

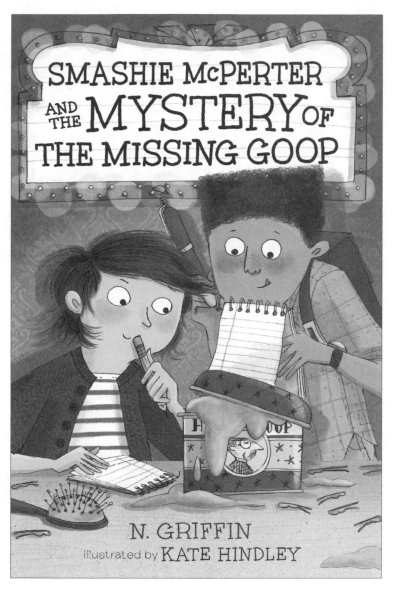

Available in hardcover and paperback and as an e-book